# Innocent Blood

## A Story of Redemption

### Sultana Jones

Edited and Designed by Rootskybooks.com
www.rootskybooks.com

First Edition

Printed in the United States of America

If you have any questions or concerns, please write to:
letsprosper2@gmail.com


www.xulonpress.com

# What They Are Saying

"Very powerful and well-written." — April Selenskikh

"Outstanding." — Tana! Angie

"You will not only begin to weigh the heavy issue in your mind, but prayerfully this book will help you understand that a life, God's people, are very important and they are more than just a fetus. That there is a living human being that is shaped in the mother's womb and there is purpose and destiny in that life." — Andre Knighton CEO, God's Child Multimedia Productions

"A remarkable story about how one stillborn fetus changed a man's life. It shows how quickly God can change our life through touching our hearts, mind, body, and soul." — Derek Boyd Hankerson, M.A., Producer WFOY/Newstalk 1240AM and ESPN 1420 AM

"The acknowledgement that Jesus Christ will redeem everyone that repents from their sin and brings restoration to their broken life is a liberating reality that is highlighted in this book." — Gregory Magruder

"The story Innocent Blood really touched me because of a bad experience as a teen. I had been raped and had gotten pregnant. My mother encouraged me to have an abortion, and I did. Reading this book brought back real memories, and to know there is redemption for me is a blessing. Thank you for writing it." — Betty Johnson

"This book gives a perfect picture of the gruesome horror of abortions and the deception of those that are involved in performing these murderous acts on precious innocent babies." — W. Clore Dice, former crisis pregnancy center director

This book is dedicated to my children,
Analea and Edward, God's gift to me

# Contents

# Acknowledgments

I want to first thank God for giving me this book in a dream, and then I want to thank John my husband for being the wind in my sails and putting up with all the late night typing. Then I want to thank Terrie Walters for believing in this book and it's message. And for my sister Zelda who prayed for me into the wee hours thanks for the covering sis.

# CHAPTER 1

# In the Beginning

Angry faces lined the street. Glaring and chanting. I saw them every day ... and I still was not used to it. Our clients seemed to come in regardless of the pleas for them to turn around.

Judy, my receptionist, was good at making the clients feel at ease. She was redheaded, light and bubbly, with a skill at running the office like no one I've ever met. I worked at a women's clinic ... a very successful one at that.

My partners, Bill and Ted, were a little rough around the edges. They weren't at first! I had been fresh out of med school, had gone through residency as an obstetrician, and was going into pediatrics when I met Bill. He had hair, then. He was tall and thin, with a bushy mustache that looked more like a pet than anything else.

He offered me a partnership, and I accepted it. Work was relentless, yet rewarding. I liked delivering babies, and it was only a few years later when Ted came on board. He just seemed to fit right in. We flowed together. We had a great team and we knew it.

Ted was about 5'10" tall, clean-cut and full of humor. The clients loved him — at least in the beginning. Ted was always full of new ideas, and I was, like, the "mastermind" who could make it happen. Bill was more laid-back and made sure we didn't go overboard. Together we rose to be one of the top pediatric clinics around. It was nothing to see our names written in well-known magazines or hospital journals!

We were sitting down one day having dinner — going over new ideas — when Ted mentioned the women's clinic. "This is where America is going, and this is where the money is," he said, taking both Bill and me in with his glance.

"Nationwide last year, this 'industry' took in over a billion dollars — so why shouldn't we get in on the game?"

Bill and I glanced at each other. What Ted said made sense. We nodded. We all agreed. So we closed down the pediatric clinic and, the rest is, well, what it is. Who would have thought that I would be on the other end of pediatrics?

I was nervous at first, when in walked my first client: A young girl, 16 years old, blonde hair, very pretty; she was five months pregnant. She was with her mother, a heavy-set woman with dirty, blonde hair, who looked to be about in her upper thirties.

"She tried to hide that she was pregnant! Now tell me, how long do you think that would have worked? I told her to 'Leave that boy alone' and asked her, 'Where is he now?'"

The girl looked down with shame. I took them back toward the examining room. "Ma'am, I have to ask you to go out in the waiting room; we will call you back when we get through."

"But, I want—"

I cut the mother off gently, but firmly. "I'm sorry, ma'am. It's the policy."

Frustrated, the mom turned around and left.

As soon as she did, I heard a very timid voice saying, "Thank you."

Now how do you say relax to a child that you are about to perform an abortion on? I glanced at the nurse, as if expecting her to answer the question that had been floating around my head. I was glad she was there!

I turned back to the girl and cleared my throat. "This is not going to hurt much," I lied. I avoided her wide eyes as I mumbled another lie that I hoped was reassuring, "It's just a piece of tissue."

I took a deep breath. "You'll feel so much better when this is over," I said, but I wasn't sure if I was trying to reassure her or me.

"Just scoot down to the end of the table, please."

My nurse handed me the needle that caused the girl to begin to contract, which made the blood begin to flow.

I have smelled blood before while delivering babies, but this was different: It was not just the blood. It was the sound of the vacuum that we used in some procedures. We had state-of-the-art equipment, which made pulling apart each piece of the tiny "tissue matter" quicker...an arm, head, legs, and the torso...lastly the sac tissue. The nurse made the final check to be sure I had gotten the entire fetus and began to clean up the "mess," so to speak.

I knew it hurt the girl, but I had nothing to say. She just sat there crying as I walked out the door. I felt sick that day, that week, in fact. It was weeks before I was able to get her look of sadness out of my head. Sleep was hard to come by, but that, too, begins to wear off with time. Even the hardest criminals can sleep after enough time goes by!

It's been six years now and I can't even count how many abortions I have performed. Unfortunately, I can now understand why Bill and Ted are the way they are – rough on the outside. Just coming into this place day after day can change anyone; well, maybe not Judy.

Looking out the window, my mind drifted to when I was a child. I don't remember too much of my childhood, only that Dad had a good job working for the government and Mom stayed home and took care of me. It's a little foggy on what went wrong with Mom and Dad. I do remember something about Dad drinking, and Mom and him fighting. I can't be certain, but it seemed like they fought over every little thing.

Later, I remember that Mom started drinking, too, and Dad would come home later and later. Many times, I would hear them yelling and knocking over things. Sometimes Dad wouldn't come home at all, and Mom would just sit in her dark bedroom drinking and crying.

•

The only person who ever came to the house was Mom's sister, Aunt Deb.

"You've got to get out of this house," Aunt Deb would tell my mom. But my mom would only look sad.

Aunt Deb would press. "Jesus loves you," she would say. "He does not want you to live like this."

One day, my mom finally accepted an invitation to attend church with Aunt Deb. Dad didn't care too much for Aunt Deb. He called her a "fanatic," but I loved her.

She was fun to be around and always had a little surprise to give me. Before long, Mom started going with Aunt Deb to church on a regular basis.

Dad never wanted to go to church, and I was caught in the

middle. He never let me go. After Mom started going to those meetings, she stopped fighting back with Dad.

But that wasn't the end of the drama between my parents. It got much worse, although I don't know the details. All I know is that after whatever it was that happened, I was put into a foster home. And after I saw the judge and talked with him, I never saw my mom or dad again.

My foster dad was quite kind to me. In fact, we would play for hours, and I, of course, was the doctor. He is the one who inspired me to be a doctor.

"Excuse me, Doctor Clint," the receptionist interrupted my trip down memory lane. "You've got a call on Line 2. It's a 'Mr. Isaiah.'"

I quickly shook the old thoughts from my mind. "Tell him I will be right there!" I moved to answer the phone. "Isaiah! How are you?"

I glanced quickly at my calendar. September 6th. "I was expecting you tomorrow! Did your flight get in early?"

I listened to his reply, and then said, "You have a seminar in the Martin Building? I would love to sit in! Great! I will see you there!"

One thing about Isaiah being a Hebrew scholar: He knew what he was talking about. He would argue religion with the best of the best! He was short in stature, with grayish, brown hair. In fact, he had more hair on his chin than on the top of his head! A brilliant man, Isaiah was also a wonderful friend and mentor. I chuckled to myself. I wasn't a religious person, but I did have a few questions to ask Isaiah.

# CHAPTER 2

# 'The Voice'

ɔck at my door brought me back to the fact that I
ɑs about to perform another exam.

"Yes?"

ɔur 3 o'clock is here, Dr. Clint."

washed my hands. There sat a young African-American
ι…a face I recognized; she had been here twice before. She
ɑs light brown in color, with nut-brown hair, tattoos everywhere…and confident.

I opened her file. "Nasheeka Coleman, how are you doing?"

"Pregnant."

"I can see that," I said. "Let's see how far along you are."

She looked me straight in the eyes. "I think I'm six or
seven months!" She rolled her eyes. "I thought about keeping
the baby, but the jerk left me and gave me the money to have
an abortion on the way out. He said that it was cheaper than
child support."

Her tone is flat. "Anyway, I didn't want to get stuck taking
care of his baby, so," she paused, "here I am."

"Okay," I said, walking to her. "Well, you know the rou-
tine."

I took hold of the light so I could check out her protruding
belly. "Hmm, you feel pretty tight."

She winced. "Just relax," I reminded her.

I finished examining her. "I think we are dealing with more
than one here."

"You mean twins?" She asked me. "Oh, great! Will it cost
me more?"

"No. You may have a little more discomfort, and it might
take a little longer," I answered.

The nurse had everything ready to proceed. She handed
me the prepared needles.

"Okay, scoot down a little more. That's good. Now you are
going to feel a little discomfort."

I carefully injected her and it numbed her enough to start.
She held the table; I began to work. Soon the blood began to
flow, and I took the first little fetus. It was almost whole, and
right behind it was another little body. It opened its mouth

20

and eyes almost to look at me. Its fingers grabbed mine. And then it was still.

I quickly gave both over to the nurse, who would look through everything carefully and examine for body parts. I could tell one was a male and the other female. I felt sickened by what had just happened.

The young girl's attitude was even worse: Before I closed the door, I heard her say, "Thank you, Dr. Clint. Now I don't have to worry about day care!"

I shut the door. "Judy, I'm leaving. Cancel the rest of my appointments for today and tomorrow!"

I was used to dodging the glaring remarks, but they seemed to bother me more than ever that day! One remark in particular stuck to me and seemed to hunt me down. It came from a kind-looking woman, as I was getting into my car. She said, "Jesus held your hand today, because he loves you."

I almost stumbled as I climbed into the car. I quickly got in and sped away.

Shaken, I drove to my home in silence. Not even music could drown out what had just happened. The woman's words haunted me!

Jesus held your hand today. Jesus held your hand today. Jesus held your hand today.

The words kept repeating in my head. I could see the face of the fetus that I had just aborted, and I could feel her little touch.

I shook my head to clear away the thoughts, but they would not leave me alone. I walked to the liquor cabinet, but stopped. No, I would not drink. Jesus held your hand today. Jesus held your hand today. Jesus held –

I quickly grabbed a glass and poured rum over ice cubes. I sighed. How had I let this happen? Why did I become an abortion doctor?

I took the glass and sat down in an armchair in front of the television. I flicked on the news. Maybe the negative reports would push aside my bad thoughts.

"Clint, why do you persecute me?"

I jumped up with a start, and realized I had fallen asleep.

I jumped up and looked around the house. It was 3 a.m. The question must have been part of a dream, but why was I dreaming about persecution? And who was I persecuting?

Unable to go back to sleep, I hopped into the shower.

I shook off the question and dream, and plunged myself again into the news. The day came quickly.

Eager to see Isaiah, I headed to the Martin Building downtown. The auditorium was packed with men and women — young and old — all seemingly very professional. Isaiah was sitting on the platform and saw me walk in. He came down and greeted me and took me to a seat in the front. "I want you to have a good seat, my friend!" His handshake was strong and welcoming, compared to the hard glares and stares that I was used to getting.

I settled in. He opened with, "I am glad you all are here! Now, our minute brain, in all its understanding, is nothing compared to a single word of the Creator's voice. 'Let there be...'"

Isaiah went on to captivate us for hours with his intelligence, wit, and insight. At the end of his presentation, he stopped and said, "I will see you all back here tomorrow to conclude."

The place erupted with applause. The crowd seemed to immediately close in around him, as audience members rushed to compliment him and ask questions.

I caught his eye and he signaled for me to come over.

"Incredible! Isaiah," I said, walking to him. "You amaze me. I don't understand how you know what you know!"

In true Isaiah fashion, he smiled and said, "And I, my friend, don't understand how you know what you know."

We both laughed. "But for now, let's get something to eat," he said. "I'm starving!"

Isaiah turned to the crowd, said a few words and excused himself, promising to answer more questions the next day. We eventually extricated ourselves and found some place close to eat.

"So, Isaiah, do you believe all this stuff you teach?" I asked after we sat at the table.

22

"The question, Clint, is—," he paused, "Not what I believe. That, my friend, is inconsequential. We—"

I interrupted. "But your debates are so strong! So powerful! I feel as if I am the one debating you!"

"Correct!" Isaiah smiled broadly. "And that's what I want you to feel ... that you can hear God the Creator's voice!"

The server placed our orders on the table.

"You know, it's funny you say that. I did have something happen to me that was a bit 'strange.' To tell the truth, it shook me up a bit." I quickly looked around the restaurant.

"Really? Please elaborate."

"I performed an abortion on a young girl yesterday ..."

I paused.

"Go on."

"Well, it was two fetuses: The first one was delivered as normal, but the second one was, well, still alive. It yawned and opened its eyes; then it grabbed my finger."

Isaiah's expression did not change. He asked, "What happened next?"

"It stopped moving, and I gave it to my nurse." I took a sip from my glass of tea.

"Okay," Isaiah said. "Well, I am sure that you have had misfortunes other than this. What shook you up so much?"

"I went home that day early. Outside, a woman walked up to me and said something like, 'Jesus held your hand today because He loves you.' Okay? Then later that night I was awakened to a voice."

"What voice? What did it say?"

I almost didn't want to utter the words out loud. "This sounds crazy!"

"Go on, Clint," Isaiah urged. He took a bite of his food.

I squirmed in my seat a little and cleared my throat. "Well, it said, 'Why do you persecute Me?'"

Isaiah's face went a little pale for a second.

"What is it?" I asked.

"May I ask you a question?" Isaiah said.

"Shoot!" I took a bite of my sandwich.

"Have you ever read the Bible or gone to church?"

"Come on, Isaiah! You know me better than to ask me that!"

I was taken aback a little by the question.

"I'm sorry, Clint. I only ask because I read a similar thing in the Christians' Holy Bible."

"What do you mean?"

"In the Bible, one of the teachers of the law wanted to bring all the Christians of that day under arrest."

"So, what does that got to do with me and what I heard?"

"Well, he would hunt them down and drag them to jail, or have them killed. Story has it that a bright light shined down on him. And a voice spoke to him, saying, 'Why do you persecute me?' Then Saul said, 'Who are you, Lord?' 'I am Jesus whom you are persecuting.'"

"So, are you saying that this is what's happening to me? Isaiah, this is crazy everyone knows that the Bible isn't real!" I gave him a look of disbelief.

"I'm not saying if it is real or not. I'm saying what it says. Hey, I'll look it up and let you know what I find out, all right?"

I thought his idea was wild, but nodded. We went on to discuss other matters as we completed our meal.

"Look, where are you staying? Downtown?"

"Yes, at the Little Hotel," Isaiah said as we walked out of the restaurant.

"At least they have you in the finest hotel in town." I said to him with a smile. . Hop in I will give you a lift."

He smiled. "Oh, thank you! Will you be at the seminar tomorrow?"

"Wouldn't miss it for the world!"

The next day the place was packed. There were no seats left. Thank goodness I knew the speaker, who had a seat waiting for me in the front! When Isaiah began to speak you could hear a pin drop. "From which side of the tree of good and evil are you eating? What are you searching for, and how deep are you willing to dig for the truth?" Those words "How deep are you willing to dig for the truth" seemed to stick in my head. Before I knew it, the crowd had erupted into applause again and it was over.

This time I waited for about an hour as people surrounded Isaiah with questions. I was no different; I had a few of my own! He took one look at me and said, "You look puzzled, my friend. What is it?"

I waved off his question so he could finish answering the questions of the people surrounding him. The crowd eventually disappeared.

"Let's get out of here and go grab something to eat," Isaiah said as he gathered his papers.

"You buying?"

He laughed. "Wouldn't have it any other way."

"Then I'm in!"

This time I headed down to a little dive called Mama's Place. The food was home-cooked by a sweet little African-American woman and her family.

"You must have not liked the seminar."

I chuckled, "Don't let the outside fool you. This is the best food in town."

We grabbed a seat in the corner and started to talk. "I am being confronted by something. It's bugging me!"

"Go on."

"Look at me, Isaiah, I am a well-off, thriving doctor and I am looking for something called 'truth'!"

He looked at me over his glasses and said, "Maybe the truth you are looking for is not a something."

"Now I know I am puzzled! What are you talking about?"

"What if the truth is not a something? Or maybe not even a frame of mind. What if the truth is a 'Who'?"

The waitress interrupted us when she brought us our food. She looked at me and smiled; a look I have seen before. Her eyes were big and black like onyx, and sparkled as the night sky. Her skin was mahogany brown, young and beautiful. I smiled back and was lost for a second in her sweetness.

Once she was gone I looked at Isaiah and asked, "What are you talking about?"

"Ah, my friend, that is up to you to dig for."

"You puzzle me, Isaiah! At times you seem like you believe

this stuff that you teach, and at other times you seem as crazy as a loon."

He looked up from his tasty dish and smiled. "And yet," he pointed his finger, "they keep coming back."

We both laughed.

"What time is your flight?"

"4 p.m."

"Then where to next? November New York, then in May it's Maine?"

"I see you've read my itinerary."

"You may see me in Maine," I said, savoring the last bite of my food. "I have a cottage there. And I was planning my vacation about then."

"Great! We will talk further on this subject. Now I have a plane to catch," Isaiah said as he looked around the restaurant. "And remind me to eat here more often. This was one of the best meals I have eaten in a long while."

We left a large tip, and as I was leaving, our young waitress gave me her phone number. I told her I would call her. I put her name into my pocket and left. Isaiah smiled.

"I stopped getting numbers a while ago; count it a blessing!" We both laughed.

# CHAPTER 3

# Conflict

M onday came quickly and I was in my office early, before the crowd came. I looked at the plan for the day,
and saw that I had three abortions on the chart, not
including the walk-ins. Ted popped his head in my office and
asked, "You okay?"

"Yeah, sure. Why do you ask?"

"You've been acting a little strange, that's all," he said with
a shrug. "You don't seem to be yourself. You want to talk?"

I set aside the paper in my hand. "I've got a few minutes.
Come in."

"Ted, how do you deal with live deliveries?"

"Ah, you've had one, I take it?"

"Yes. Last Thursday. It didn't live long; seconds really.
Long enough to yawn. It opened its eyes and held my finger.
I looked at her; then she died."

"That's a hard one," Ted said. "It's happened to me plenty
of times. You get used to it. I can't tell you how many fetuses
I have delivered alive. I just wrap them up and put them in
the back room until they expire. That's all."

"That's all!?"

"Look, just think about the injustice you are sparing that
fetus!"

"Injustice?" I glanced at him quizzically.

"Yes, injustice! Years of welfare...being dragged around
by some spoiled selfish teenager...Women who don't want
to work, but want to live off the government. Clint, we have
helped so many women make the right choice! In our field
there will be risks, and one of those risks is a live delivery!
We both know the higher the trimester they are in, the higher
the risk of a live abortion. So," he reached over and picked up
the scissors, "take care of it before the fetus is delivered."

"You mean puncture before delivery?" I could not keep the
shock off my face.

"'Late term' is what we say to keep a malpractice lawsuit
off our hands!"

"I know that, but ..."

"But what?"

"It doesn't mean I like it!"

"Like has nothing to do with it! I don't like it either, Clint! But I do it! It's what the patient wants!"

Ted stood up. "And, it's good business!

He cleared his throat and his tone changed. "Look, it's time to start. Let's talk after work. Come over for dinner. Peg won't mind and the kids love to see you. What do you say?"

I nodded my head. "All right."

The day was gone before I knew it. I had performed four abortions and turned one away. All in all, it seemed like it was a good day.

But why was it bothering me so much? Not like when I first started; this was different somehow ... deeper. I hope I'm not losing my nerve!

Ted lived in a very well to-do neighborhood. His house was huge and beautiful, and the yard was always impeccable — always well groomed, always perfect. He had a cute little family: three kids — two boys and a girl, blond — and his wife, Peggy. Peg was the perfect mom! She could cook, clean and she ran a tight ship. She had blonde hair that glimmered in the light, a small, shapely body...and she was a joy to be around. Ted was right: I did enjoy coming over. It was always light and refreshing from a hard day's work. How Ted switched from "work mode" to "home mode," I'll never know.

I pulled up to the circular driveway, got out and rang the bell. I was welcomed by the excitement of three little faces and a "Come on in!" by Peggy.

"Where's Ted?"

"Oh, he's upstairs in his office and said he will be right down."

"Really? What's he up to?"

"I don't know; you know him — he's always working on something."

We chuckled. "You're right on that one."

I held out a bottle of Caymus Reserve 1991. "This is for you!"

She looked at me with a sweet and welcoming smile. "Um-m-m, my favorite! Clint, you know better; you'll spoil me."

We walked into the kitchen and I started peeking into pots

on the stove.

"What's for dinner? It smells great!" She smacked my hand away.

"It could be an old shoe, and you'd love it!"

"If you cooked it, I would eat it! You know I don't get home-cooked meals that often."

"Uncle Clint, I'm going to marine camp this summer. I'm going to study about whales."

"You are? That's great!" I was looking into the face of Ted's first-born, Terry. He was 11 years old.

"Are you excited?" I grinned at him.

Peggy piped in. "Is he excited? He has been packed for three weeks, and he doesn't leave until July!"

I roughed up his hair a little and pretended to put him in a headlock.

We wrestled for a moment until two other excited-to-see-me kids jumped me. They wrestled me down to the kitchen floor.

"Now take that to the sitting room!" Peggy said.

We stopped. The kids bounded off.

"You're as bad as the kids!" she said with a smile and shake of her head.

I stood up, tossing her a kitchen towel and said, "No, I'm worse!"

Ted walked in. "Is he wrestling in the kitchen again, Peg?"

"You know him better than I do!"

We all laughed. Peggy turned to pull a dish from the oven.

"Dinner's almost ready. Go wash up!"

We all sat down to a wonderful meal of chicken Cordon Bleu, wild rice with almonds, roasted fennel and homemade bread. After dinner, we had shaved Sherry ices. "Peggy, if you weren't already taken I would ask you to marry me! This was a great meal. Thank you."

"My pleasure, Clint, you are always welcome."

The kids bounded out and Ted and I headed into the library to talk. We shut the door. Now, Ted was not a religious person, although he and his family occasionally attended an Episcopal Church. Many of the church members have, for one reason or another, come into his office. One time, the pastor's wife came in for an abortion ... after hours.

"So what's on your mind?" Ted said as we sat down. "You're not losing your nerve now, are you?"

"No, no, it's nothing like that." I waved off the question.

"Then, what is it? One of us?"

"No, I can't quite put my finger on it," I said, biting my lip in thought. "It's a lot of things ... nothing absolute. But I do know it started with this one live abortion I performed."

"We all have those, Clint!"

"I know, Ted, but it's what followed that shook me up!"

"What was it?"

I drew in a deep breath. "I left early that day. On the way out a kind, little old lady said to me that 'Jesus loved me, and that's why He held my hand today!'"

"Okay. So, those kinds of people say anything out of their mouths." Ted leaned back in his chair and put his feet on the desk.

"Yeah, but later that night I was awakened by a voice saying, 'Clint, why do you persecute Me?'"

Ted looked at me and said, "What does that mean?"

"I don't know, but I keep hearing it – sometimes at odd times. I think I'm losing it sometimes."

"Have you talked to anybody about it?"

"Yes. Isaiah."

Ted's brows shot up in surprise. "The Isaiah? The Scholar? How do you know him? I've read all his books. He sure knows how to put those fanatics in their place!"

"We go way back. I've known him for years now. I mentioned it to him and he turned pale."

"Pale? What do you mean?"

"He said that it was something in the Bible. Look, I don't know. He said he would talk to me later after he researched more about it."

Ted nodded. "How can I help?"

I asked, "Are you religious?"

"No, no, God no!"

"Then why do you go to church?"

He shrugged. "My wife does and I want my family to be together, so I go."

Ted looked at me straight in the eyes. "You're not getting into 'abortion is the wrong thing,' are you?"

"No! But something is bugging me, that's for sure."

Ted walked over to where I was sitting. "Clint, abortion is business! So what is it?"

"I ... I don't know!"

He grabbed me by my arms. "Get a hold of yourself, Clint! You are the sharpest one of us and you know your stuff! Don't throw it away for some voice!"

I looked at him sharply and shook loose. "I'm not throwing anything away!"

He stepped back. "I'm sorry, Clint, I don't know why I did that. I just saw everything crumbling around us, that's all."

"It's all right. I know the feeling." We stood in silence for a beat.

Ted cleared his throat. "Look, it's late and we have a busy day tomorrow."

I stood and walked toward the door. Ted quickly strode behind me and snatched open the door.

Peggy was standing there when it opened. She had heard the conflict.

"Is everything all right?" she asked, looking from Ted to me. Ted and I exchanged awkward glances and nodded.

I gave Peggy a hug. "Thanks again for dinner."

I left.

# CHAPTER 4

# A New Man

The drive home was as empty as they come. Never before had Ted and I had a confrontation like that one! Sure, we disagreed, but never like this.

I hopped out of the car and quickly walked into the house. I could hear every step I made, and my keys unlocking the door seemed louder than ever. I closed the door. I looked at the clock: 9:30. I sat down in silence; I was filled with anger, hurt and confusion. I walked over to my wall by my bookcase and over it was a photo of the three of us, Bill, Ted, and me standing in the old pediatrician's office. Why did this photo bother me? What's going on in my head? I wish Isaiah were here now. He has such wisdom. Of course he left me with enough to think on.

The phone rang. It was Ted. "Hello?"

"I want to say I'm sorry for what happened tonight."

"I understand. No problem," my tone was conciliatory. "Let's just put this all behind us, Ted You're a great doctor, a great pediatrician."

"Yeah, that was before and now we are going places!" He added, "I just want to make sure you're going with us."

I paused for a moment and then struggling, said, "Yeah, yeah, look I'm kind of tired, see you tomorrow."

"Sure thing. Tomorrow."

I hung up and felt hollow inside. The next day I plunged into work and turned off any feelings that tried to surface. I continued that way for some time. Many nights the voice would keep me awake, and sometimes I would yell to the emptiness of my apartment.

One time I was on a date when the voice spoke to me and I hollered for it to stop bothering me. The woman I was with jumped up and left quickly.

I didn't blame her. I would have, too. It's been four months since I started hearing the voice. I can't take it anymore! I've got to have some answers.

On the counter, from a pocket of odds and ends that I had emptied out months ago — lay the paper with a phone number on it. I smiled: It was the number the little waitress had given me in front of Isaiah. I picked up the phone, took a deep breath, and dialed. I was hoping that she would pick up.

It rang. "Come on, pick up!"

It rang again. I was just about to hang up when.

"Hello?"

"Ah-h-h, hello? Is this Katrina?"

"Yes, it is." I felt a bit awkward. I never have trouble asking a girl out, but for some reason this felt different.

"Ah-h-h, this is Clint. You gave me your number at the restaurant."

"I remember. I was hoping that you would call. How are you?"

I let out a tiny breath. I didn't realize I had been holding it. "I'm fine ... fine. Um, look, I was wondering," I paused, "if you would like to meet me tonight?"

"Sure, where?"

"How about the Robin's Roost, say, in an hour?"

"That sounds great! See you there."

Suddenly my spirit picked up and I started to get ready. I changed into some jeans and a black T-shirt. I heard the voice again: "Clint, Why Do You Persecute Me?"

I stumbled back, knocking over a plant that was on the counter. I put my hands over my ears, but it did not help. I grabbed my keys and left. In the car I turned the music up to drown out those words ... that seemed to echo inside my head.

I reached the Robin's Roost first and went inside, waiting for Katrina to come in. The songs beat with the lights. The place was loud and smoke-filled. I needed answers! I am a logical person, and something illogical was happening to me. I needed some answers quick. I don't pray; never ever have I prayed before. But for some reason, in this loud environment I uttered my first weak prayer: "God, give me some answers!"

Katrina walked in. She was a beautiful sight to see. She was dressed in jeans with a pink top. Her hair lay on her shoulders, giving her a sweetness that accented her smile. I walked over to her and extended my hand. She gently took

35

mine as I led her to our table. "Why did you come?"

She smiled. "Why did you call?"

"I don't know, really," I admitted. "I was looking for something."

I went back to my original question. Why did you come?"

"I felt that you needed answers."

I did a double take. "Excuse me?"

"I felt God say to go to you."

I ignored the reference to God. "Let's order. Are you hungry?"

"A little. Maybe just an appetizer for me. Chips and spinach dip sounds good."

I singled to the waiter, who came right over. "What can I get for you?"

I placed our orders. "She will have the chips and spinach dip and I would like the Buffalo wings, please."

I glanced at the menu. "Oh and two ice teas?"

Katrina nodded her head and smiled.

I shifted in my seat. "So tell me how long you've been working at Mama's Place?"

Her smile was enchanting. "Let's say I washed my first pot of greens standing in a chair."

"Really? That young? So you can cook, huh?"

"You might say that. I noticed you like homemade biscuits. I've been making those since I was seven."

"I must have eaten five of them myself and Isaiah ate three that day. Boy they were good!"

I think she blushed. "Thank you, I believe I'm a master at making them by now."

"Would you be willing to teach me?"

"The art of biscuit making?" She giggled. "Sure, I'd love to."

"So it's a date then. Let's say, tomorrow?"

"If you're brave enough to come I'm brave enough to teach you. Yes, it's a date."

•

Katrina and I started hanging out whenever she was not working. It was the best two weeks of my life, until one night it happened, I was with Katrina on our way to dinner and the voice spoke to me, I threw my hands over my ears and shouted "STOP IT!" Katrina froze.

"What is it, Dr. Clint? Stop what?" We were on our way to the Robin's Roost. I know she thought I was crazy.I regained my composure. "Look, are you hungry?"

"Not really. I just ate."

I looked around. "Could we skip the Robin's Roost and go walking downtown?"

"Sure."

She climbed into my Mercedes and we drove off.

"So, what's going on with you? You looked like you were in pain?"

I didn't say anything for a moment. "I need to know something Are you," I paused. "A ... a Christian?"

"Yes, I am." She laughed.

"What?"

"I thought you were going to ask some hard question. Why did you ask?"

"Well, don't think I'm crazy, but," I paused again. "I keep hearing voices. Well, not really voices, but one voice. It doesn't matter where I am — at work or at home. I could be driving or watching TV, and I still hear it! It's making me nuts!"

I waited for her to slowly back away, but she just sat there and listened. "What does it say?"

I parked the car under a light downtown. We got out. People were coming and going, looking at the shops. We sat on a bench.

"Should I ask you again?" She smiled.

"No." I smiled at her and paused again.

She was patient. "The voice says, 'Clint, why do you persecute me?'"

"Who or what is asking me this?" I asked. "A friend told me that this is from a story in the ... the—,"

"Bible," she completed my sentence.

"And?"

"Yes, it is."

"If this is true, then this 'voice,' *who* or *what* is it? Why is it haunting me?"

I had no idea how Katrina would react. I was embarrassed. She reached into her purse and pulled out a small, black Bible. "I didn't know why I needed this, but now I understand why."

She looked at me with a sweetness I could feel in my soul. "Could I say a little prayer first?" I nodded my head. "Dear God, tonight please give Clint the answer he's looking for. Amen!"

She turned to me. "In the Bible, there is a man named Saul. He was devoted to keeping the old laws. He—"

"My friend mentioned the same story." I apologized for interrupting. "I'm sorry. Go on."

" You see, they had put Jesus Christ to death years before, but God raised Him from the dead, and there were many eye-witnesses that this happened. But the guards who guarded the tomb of Jesus were paid to say someone took him in the middle of the night. Jesus appeared to many people after that."

"Go on."

"Well, after this, the Jewish leaders tried to stamp out the conversion of the people to Jesus."

"Why?"

"Because He was real! He was alive! The story is found in the Book of Acts, Chapter 9, verse 1."

She situated the Bible on her lap and started reading. *"Then Saul, still breathing threats and murder against the disciples of the Lord, went to the high priest and asked him for letters from him to the synagogues of Damascus, so that if he found any who were of the Way, whether men or women, he might bring them bound to Jerusalem. As he journeyed he came near Damascus, and suddenly a light shown around him from heaven. Then he fell to the ground, and heard a voice saying to him, 'Saul, Saul, why are you persecuting me?'"*

I pointed at the book in her lap. "That's just like the voice I heard! What happened next?"

*"Let's see," she paused. "Oh here we go, 'Who are You, Lord?' Then the Lord said, 'I am Jesus, whom you are perse-*

cuting ... *Arise and go into the city, and you will be told what you must do.' And the men who journeyed with him stood speechless, hearing a voice but seeing no one. Then Saul arose from the ground, and when his eyes were opened he saw no one. But they led him by the hand and brought him into Damascus. And he was three days without sight, and neither ate nor drank."*

I interrupted her. "You mean Jesus Christ, *the* Jesus Christ," I paused again. "Has been talking to me all this time? But why? How am I persecuting Him? I mean ... I thought I was a good person. I help out in the community when I can, or at least I give a large check to different charities every year. I'm nice to people or at least I try to be nice. See I'm a good person. What have I done to have Him speak to me like this?"

"I don't know, but Saul was having the innocent Christians killed. He said that Saul was doing it to him."

Katrina took hold of my hand and said, "Jesus says that if you did this to the least of *them*, you have done it unto *me*."

As she took hold of my hand, my heart sank inside of me... tears began to well up in my throat. I could see the little baby in my hands, and feel her touch all over again. I could hear Ted's cold voice when he grabbed me and said that abortion is just a business. Katrina's sweet voice was the final blow to my heart. "Clint, whatever it is, Jesus is real! You've heard Him yourself. He will forgive you, and He will use you like He went on to use Saul, who is now called Paul."

I couldn't hide the tears. They flowed freely now. "You don't understand, Katrina, I am a doctor who ... who performs ..."

She interrupted, "Abortions."

"Yes, but how did you know?"

"I was one of those girls!"

"What?" My eyes were wide.

"I came in and you didn't even look at me. You performed the abortion and left. The nurse cleaned me up. That was years ago, and I gave my heart to Jesus at Mama's Place."

I swallowed hard. "Oh God, what have I done?"

"Ask Jesus to forgive you of this sin."

"How can I? I've shed so much innocent blood."

She touched my arm lightly then held up that Bible.

"How could Saul? It starts with repentance."

I searched her face for answers. "I feel like my heart's going to explode. It hurts so much."

"Let's pray and ask Jesus to forgive you of your sins, and for Him to come into your heart."

Right there on the bench I repented, and asked Jesus to come into my heart. There was so much inside, that I just couldn't stop weeping. Case after case came up to my mind. Oh God, I've taken so many little lives. I could hear a page being turned with each one I repented for and gave over to Him. I kept doing this until I heard a new voice; it said, "Be at peace now; all is done."

It felt as if we had been kneeling there for hours. Katrina must have thought that I lost my mind. I just heard Him say, "Peace — all is done!"

I grabbed her and hugged her tightly! I stood up and shouted, "Thank You, God! Thank You!"

Then I fell to my knees ... weeping again. Katrina covered me like a mother would cover her baby. I got up from that spot a new man. A *free* man!

# CHAPTER 5

# The Time of Testing

Monday morning, I woke up to my 7:45 alarm. I took my shower, and this thought hit my mind: *What will Bill and Ted think? What are they going to say? Should I quit? How do I tell them? Oh, by the way, I am a Christian now!*

Question after question began to bombard my mind. It had only been a short while since my conversation with Katrina, but I saw life in such a different way. I actually embraced the idea of being a Christian — something I had never considered before that talk.

The phone rang. "Hello?"

"Hello, this is Katrina. You were on my heart, so I called."

I smiled. "Katrina, it's good to hear your voice."

"Are you okay?" I could hear the concern in her voice. "You sound a little ruffled?"

"Strange you should ask, but it seems that my brain is being hit by question after question. I wish it would stop!"

"You sound like you are under a spiritual attack." "

I wrinkled my brow. "What? I don't follow you."

"I'm sorry. Do you have the little Bible I gave you last night?"

"Yes, it's a wonderful gift."

"Turn to the book of Ephesians, Chapter 6; start at verse 11. Go to the front of the Bible for the index; you will see the page number there."

I grabbed the Bible and began looking for the passage. "Ephesians, Ephesians, Chapter 6. Okay I'm there."

"Read that for me."

*"Put on the whole armor of God, that you may be able to stand against wiles of the devil. For we do not wrestle against flesh and blood, but against principalities, against powers, against the rulers of the darkness of this age, against spiritual hosts of wickedness in the heavenly places. Therefore take up the whole armor of God, that you may be able to withstand in the evil day, and having done all, to stand.*

*"Stand therefore, having girded your waist with truth, having put on the breastplate of righteousness, and having shod your feet with the preparation of the gospel of peace; above*

*all, taking the shield of faith with which you will be able to quench all the fiery darts of the evil one. And take the helmet of salvation, and the sword of the Spirit, which is the word of God; praying always with all prayer and supplication in the Spirit, being watchful to this end with all perseverance and supplication for all the saints — and for me, that I may open my mouth boldly to make known the mystery of the gospel, for which I am an ambassador in chains; that in it I may speak boldly, as I ought to speak."*

I finished the passage. "Well, this is interesting, but how does it apply to me?"

"You see, Jesus is this armor, and He wants us to wrap ourselves completely into Himself, totally dependent upon His protection. Read your Bible every chance you get. Make the time and do it. We will pray for you at Mama's today."

"Thank you; I think that I understand what you are telling me."

I hung up the phone and made a cup of coffee. When I sat down to read, it was 8:15. The next time I looked at the clock it was 10 that morning. Something began to come alive in my heart! I felt like a school kid! I devoured that little Bible.

But I knew I had to get to work. I quickly dressed and drove to the clinic.

I felt a cold chill as I walked through the door. It seemed as if I were a stranger! It was the same desk and the same chair as before. Nothing was out of the ordinary, but I just didn't feel right. Already there were patients waiting beyond those doors for me to come in. I knew it was just a matter of time before Ted would be in my office, especially after the way I left his house.

A knock at the door made me jump; it was Ted. "Clint, may I come in?"

"Of course, Ted. Sit down. What's on your mind?"

He cleared his throat and sat down. "I think you know."

"Don't worry about it, Ted."

You could cut the uneasiness with a knife. "I don't know what got into me, Clint. I was afraid you were becoming ..." He paused.

"What?"

"… well, one of these religious freaks out there."

"And if I were," I stumbled through my words, "one of those 'religious freaks,' as you put it, then what?"

Ted stood up. "Then I would have to insist that you leave, before you can do any harm!"

I looked at him in surprise. Was he serious? He would just kick me out of the practice? Not that I was sure I wanted to stay. "Any harm? What are you talking about 'any harm?' Day after day we come into this place and tear apart unborn babies, and forever change the lives of women and children! And that is not *harm* to you? Ted, we were pediatricians — the best in the field! We brought forth live babies, not *dead* ones! What more harm can I do?!"

"You can try to tear down everything we have worked for all these years! I won't have it, you hear me!"

We both spoke in excited tones. "Ted, think about what you are saying! It is not about *money*! It is about the *lives*! God knows about every little life that is destroyed by our hands."

"Don't talk to me about God! I have worked too hard to get to where I am, and God had nothing to do with it! Don't talk to me about some *God*!"

I shot back. "You are right! God had nothing to do with this. He started you with us as pediatricians, then greed entered in!"

"This is where the money is and you know it!"

I shook my head. "Ted, the Bible says, *'For what will it profit a man if he gains the whole world, and loses his own soul'.*"

"Clint, I had respect for you, until now!" Ted leapt from his seat. "Take your … your Bible and your preaching and get the hell out of here! You can talk to me in court!"

And with that, Ted walked out the door.

I sat in silence for a while. For how long, I don't know. It could have been 20 or 30 minutes, and then I began to pack my things. Judy knocked and poked her head in the door. "May I come in?"

"Sure, come on in."

This was the first time I didn't see Judy with a smile.

"Dr. Clint, I couldn't help overhearing the conversation between you and Dr. Ted. I wasn't trying to, but I did."

I sighed. "I'm sure everyone heard it."

"No, I kind of turned up the music," she chuckled.

"Dr. Clint, tell me, is it true … did you become a Christian? And are you leaving us?" "Yes, Judy, it is true."

She studied my face. "What happened?"

"Do you really want to know?"

She nodded.

I began to tell her what had happened to me. She was only in the office with me for about ten minutes or so, but I shared Jesus with her. I didn't know all the ins and outs of my new faith, but I knew what mattered: Jesus loved me and for the first time in my life, I accepted all that He offered. Right there in my office, Judy gave her heart and life to following Jesus, just as I had done such a short time ago.

"Dr. Clint, what do I do now?"

"Pray and read the Bible. Jesus will let you know what to do next."

I handed her Katrina's phone number and said for her to call her. "It's not going to be an easy walk, but Jesus will always be by your side. We will talk soon. I just know that I can't stay and work here anymore, and Ted doesn't think so, either."

Judy looked concerned. "What will you do?"

"I'm not sure." I just could not stay in that place a second longer than necessary. Even looking around my office made my skin crawl.

With that, I picked up the box I had filled and walked out the door. The waiting room was filled with patients and I simply said, "Goodbye folks. I can no longer kill the unborn."

I could have heard a pin drop as I walked outside. Religious protestors hurled rude comments at me as I walked to the car. I wanted to defend myself and say that I had quit, but part of me felt that what they said was true and I deserved it. I got into my car and drove away. A million things flashed in my head: How long would I be out of work? I'd never been in that predicament before. I had money saved in the bank but how long would that last? I had to force my mind to shut off before worry took over.

I hadn't gone very far when my cell phone rang. "Hello? Bill, I was wondering when you were going to call me. I know you are off today."

He said a few words. "No, this wasn't a rash decision. It's deeper than that."

I listened as he spoke. I nodded, but realized he could not see. "I've got some time. Where do you want to meet? Let me guess … The Captain's Bell? When? I can be there in fifteen minutes."

I turned down a side street. "Okay I'll see you then."

I pulled up in the parking lot and there was Bill pacing back and forth, smoking a cigarette. He had a very concerned look on his face, and yet he was able to squeeze out a smile. We shook hands.

"How did you know I wanted to meet at the Captain's Bell?" He said as we walked in.

"Bill, how long have we known each other? If there is one thing I learned after all these years is that whenever you get nervous, you eat seafood."

We laughed.

They seated us at a table.

I got right to the point. "Now, I know that you have talked to Ted, right?"

Bill nodded. "I talked with him, but I didn't believe him. It just doesn't make sense, Clint! Ted tried to tell me that you got religion and that you can't work anymore. Is that true?"

"Now, you know me better than that by now, Bill, and you know that it's deeper than that." I went into everything that had happened to me. Bill listened intently, pausing only when the waitress came by with the food and drinks.

"Maybe you need some time off, Clint. Get some rest and think about this for a while."

"That's just it, Bill!" I said. "I know it's only been a very short while, but I *have* thought this out, over and over again! I know it makes no sense now, but I only hope it will one day."

Bill still looked confused and concerned. "And that's it? All those years together and this is the conclusion you have come to? Clint, you sound mad!"

I shook my head and turned the situation around on him. "No, Bill, I don't! Look at you! You used to have so much life! You used to laugh and joke around and smile! Now look at yourself; you hardly ever laugh. You are short with people, almost mean. Where is your joy now? You and your wife are on the edge of divorce and what for? The life of an unborn child! And *money*! We were pediatricians! Live babies, remember?"

Then Bill interrupted. "We all came to that decision and we all have benefited from it, if I recall."

I rubbed my hands through my hair in frustration. "Well, I don't need money stained with blood!"

Bill pointed at me with his fork. "Well that stained money bought you your condo and that nice car you drive around in. It's funny how the money is stained now but what about then? Clint, come on. You are going over the edge a bit. You can be a Christian and do this too. Lots of people do it."

I slowly shook my head no. "Bill, I've found out that God is real. And to keep doing what I was doing would be," I looked him straight in the eyes, "wrong."

"There is no logic to what you are saying, Clint! You are telling me that because of some new faith, *God* is making you throw away everything we have worked together for? Clint, won't you reconsider?"

I shook my head, "No."

Bill threw his hands in the air. "That's it, then? I guess there's no turning you."

Bill took a deep breath. I knew something else was coming. I didn't have to wait long. "Clint, Ted is going to sue you."

I nodded. "I know."

Bill cleared his throat and stood. "Then I have nothing else to say to you. We will see you in court!"

With that, Bill walked away from the table, paid the check, and left.

I sat there in silence for about a half an hour. I thought about the times we had spent together. The years I had spent with their families, their kids knowing me as "Uncle Clint." I was feeling really low about that time, but I knew that Jesus Himself asked me to stop. I would never return to that office!

The drive home seemed long. So much had happened in such a little time. I walked into my house and set my box of stuff on the table. The next morning I was awakened to a knock at the door. I opened it. Reporters crowded the doorway, taking my picture and firing questions at me.

"Is it true that you stole money from your patients?"

"What did you do with the money?"

"How long have you embezzled money?"

I held up a hand. "What? What are you talking about?"

"Dr. Clint, are you depressed?" A reporter I recognized from a local television station asked.

"No."

"What are your views on abortion now?" A female reporter asked me, jamming a microphone into my face.

"I ... I." The questions caught me off guard. I blinked into the bright lights of the cameras and looked around.

"Why did you leave?"

"Please stop! No more questions, please!"

"Is it true—"

I shoved them back and slammed my door.

Just then the phone rang. I stumbled to it, my head still spinning from what just happened.

"Hello?"

"Good morning, Sunshine!"

"Judy?"

"Yes, it's me," she lowered her voice. "I thought I'd give you a call to see what happened yesterday. Dr. Ted filled me in at the end of the day. He was also not very happy. I wonder what will happen when I give him my notice? I thought I would stay as long as I could, and talk to as many girls as I can before I get the boot. I know that when Dr. Ted and Dr. Bill find out what I'm doing, I'm history."

I took a steadying breath and glanced at the front door to

make sure I had locked it. "I'm fine; just a little shook up. I was greeted this morning by a swarm of reporters."

"I know. Dr. Ted was talking to a reporter yesterday. He says he's going to kill your reputation."

I slumped into a chair. "Great! That's all I need."

"I talked to Katrina last night, and told her what was going on. She prayed for you and me. I felt peace in my heart for the first time in a long time."

"She has that effect on people," I said with a smile. Katrina had already changed my life so much.

"Dr. Ted is really going through with this. I heard him talking to Dr. Bill. You should think about getting a lawyer. Look, I have to go. I'm at the office and my first blessing just walked through the door. I will talk to you later. Bye."

"Bye."

I could not explain the mixed emotions. Just the thought that Ted was going after me like this upset me. I ate with him! Shared his family, everything! And now he wanted to sue me? I felt a flash of anger begin to rise for a brief moment, and then it was gone. That was strange! Any other time I would have brooded over that anger for a day or two, but now I just felt pity. Plain pity.

# CHAPTER 6

# Support

The phone rang. I let the answering machine pick up. It was the Daily News wanting an interview. It rang again and again, one reporter after another. I took the phone off the hook.

I was still new to Christianity, so I wasn't sure how it all worked, but I turned to God. After all, He was the one who led me to this decision, so I thought He could help me deal with everything that was happening to me. I knelt down right there in the kitchen and prayed, "Oh God, what shall I do?"

I didn't know it would be this hard. The people I thought were my friends had turned their backs on me. The work I had held onto for so long now repulsed me. I broke down under the pressure of the past few days.

I wept. I cried until my throat felt dry and my head hurt.

I heard the ringing of my cell phone. It was Katrina. I tried to clear my throat when I answered, but she wasn't fooled.

"Dr. Clint? What's going on?"

"Oh, nothing," I said. "I was just—"

"Tell me what's wrong," she cut me off in a gentle but firm tone.

I wiped tears from my cheeks and drew in a steadying breath. "Reporters have been hounding me," I said. "People I used to work with are suing me. They are lying on me, ruining my reputation. I ... I didn't know it would be this hard. I don't know about this Christian thing. I wasn't expecting this."

"Neither did Paul! Do you remember what he went through? No one believed him, not even the Christian brothers and sisters at first. Clint, put on your armor and get ready to fight! Fight for Jesus."

"My what?"

"Do you have your little Bible near?"

"Yes, I keep it close to me now."

"Good, remember the time when you thought after thought was hitting your mind?"

"Yes it was E, Ephesians 6! So how does that apply to this?"

"Turn to Ephesians chapter 6 and read that and take God

at His word."

I felt weak, but her words gave me a newfound strength not to quit. I nodded, though I realized she could not see me.

She went on. "Do you remember what Paul did to prove he loved Jesus?"

I answered, "He went to fellowship groups and church meetings to tell them about God's great love and mercy in his life."

"That's right! The devil tried to stop him, but he couldn't and he can't stop you either, Clint! Why don't you come and speak at our church group tonight? About 7 p.m. Mama would love to see you there. Mama's Place. What do you say?"

"Okay," I said, almost surprising myself. Just a few days ago I would not have recognized Paul but he heard the voice like I did.

I hung up the phone. *I think I am crazy. What's going to happen when they hear my story? I will be hated.* What was I saying? I'm hated *now*! I chuckled to myself.

Seven arrived before I knew it. The back room at Mama's Place was packed. I looked around for Katrina, and spotted her sitting in the front. "Dr. Clint," she smiled, "I was beginning to think that you got cold feet."

"I almost did! I didn't expect this big of a turnout."

"Are you nervous?"

"I have to admit, I am," I said, sitting next to her. I have talked at plenty of conferences before, but I've never felt like this before."

"Like what?"

"A school kid, you know, just coming out of college."

Soon our attention was turned to the front of the room. Mama stood up and began to pray. I could feel a warmth come over me, the same sweetness that came over me when Katrina would pray. It was like waves and waves of liquid love. Then I heard the Voice, *His* Voice speak to me, "Tell them of my love, of my mercy, of my forgiveness. Tell them to repent, and follow Me."

"Yes, Lord. I will."

The singing echoed in my heart, and I melted in God's presence. I had no more nervousness — only a sweet reassurance that Jesus was right there next to me.

Katrina took the floor. "I have asked this brother if he would come and share his testimony with us, and he is here tonight. Dr. Edward Clint."

I walked up front to the homemade pulpit and just stood there for a minute. Then I said ...

"I am a doctor. Two other doctors and I ran a very successful pediatric office in the center of town six years ago. Unfortunately, we closed it down and opened a women's clinic instead. Not of *life*, but of *death*. I was an abortionist, until a real and loving God turned me around. Why? What would God even want with someone who has destroyed the lives of so many? I am the lowest of them all. Sure, I had money. I was driving the car of my dreams, but I was empty and I felt dirty. I would go to clubs and bars trying to drown out the abortions that I had performed that day. So why, then? Was I so special? No, something I read last night in the Bible made my heart jump inside of me. It's found in John chapter 3 number 16, *"For God so loved ..."* He so loved *me*, folks, and He loved you, that's the only reason!

"Is it that easy? No, He showed me His mercy. I didn't and I don't deserve His mercy or His love, but He gave it freely. So I ask again, is it that easy? No. There is a price that He requires, and I learned it is given through something called repentance. It's a laying down all ownership of one's life. You see, God had his hand on my life and I never knew it. It's funny. I thought I was in control of my life. I had just performed an abortion where the baby was alive briefly. It was a girl," the tears began flowing down my face as I spoke the bitter truth. "She looked at me and grabbed my finger, then died. The whole thing shook me up so bad that I left my office that day. On the way out to my car an elderly woman came up to me and said, 'Jesus loves you,' then she added, 'that's why He held your hand today.'"

I looked out over the crowd and saw several people nodding, as if encouraging me to go on. "Those words haunted me over and over again — 'Jesus loves you.' How could He? I took a shower. Then I heard, 'Clint, why are you persecuting me?'"

The crowd gasped. "It shook me up. I heard it again only louder, 'Clint, why are your persecuting me?' I heard this voice at work, driving, at the club, and at the bar. I thought I was going crazy.

"You see, I had never read the Bible before, and I had only been to church twice when I was a young boy. But God had a plan, and it wasn't long before I was on my knees, repenting. Repenting for every abortion I had committed, and every life I had ruined; repenting for every lie that I had told! Everything! I held nothing back from God. He knew me inside out. Nothing was secret — I was transparent. I have now given ownership of my life over to Jesus."

I drew in a breath. There was not a dry eye in the room. "I want you to know that Jesus is here right now, ready to forgive you if you have had an abortion. Or if you have fathered a baby and paid for an abortion. Or maybe if your daughter has had an abortion and you encouraged it or paid for it."

I felt a strange boldness. "God wants you to repent and be clean in your heart. You don't have to wait to hear a "Voice" like I did. Don't you know that you already hear that voice? Every time you hear a baby cry or see a pregnant woman or every time you see a happy child run by, that Voice gets louder and louder. Every Mother's Day or every Father's Day is a reminder that you had or encouraged an abortion. That's one thing I can say: I feel clean and He will clean you up, too. So, if that is you tonight, come on up and we will pray for you. Will you be truthful to your heart tonight?"

I stood there and no one moved. I thought, *"Oh no, this can't be good!"*

Then, down the middle aisle, came this teenage girl. She had tears flowing down her cheeks, and she knelt down. Then another and another; men and women came forward, old and young. You could hear the sound of weeping deep sobs of regret, deep sobs from the heart.

Katrina stood up and said, "Your sin has a name. So ask

God for forgiveness of each one He brings to your heart. It is called 'repentance,' and when you are done, God will tell you and you will be clean. Then ask Him to fill you up with Himself, and choose to follow Him."

The sound was agonizing. Men and women were praying with those who came forward. Every now and then you would hear a victorious shout of someone who got free. What a night! What a glorious night! When I went home, I thanked God for His faithfulness in coming tonight and for freeing hearts.

I went to bed feeling like I had accomplished something.

A phone call woke me up at 8 a.m. "Hello?"

"Hello, Dr. Clint, my name is Pastor Randolph. I pastor the Grace Community Hall in Portsmouth County."

He paused. "I heard about the meeting you had last night at the restaurant. I was hoping you would come and speak here, too. This Friday at 7 p.m.?"

My phone rang again. It was another pastor, asking the same thing for Saturday night. All that morning I was getting calls to come to speak. I said I would get back in touch with them. I called Katrina and told her what was going on.

"That is amazing!" she said. "God is showing great favor."

"So you think I should do it?"

"Oh, yes," she said. "You have a story to tell and lives to touch."

So, I began to go to the churches and meeting halls to speak about what God had done in my life. God would pour Himself out mightily and change hearts. I was always careful not to take any of His work to my credit. This was God and God alone who was touching hearts.

Pastor Randolph became a big supporter and friend. He had a love for the unborn and the lost. He was full of wisdom and very humble, and he didn't have to yell to get his point across or to expose you of sin. I enjoyed Pastor Randolph. We spent the holiday months together. He took time to sit with me, open up the Bible, and answer questions I had that were locked inside of me. I grew quickly in Jesus and His word. Judy enjoyed listening, too! She also met Pastor Randolph's son, Mark and they hit it off almost as if they knew each other for years. It was funny that Mark's hair was as red as Judy's. I chuckled when I saw them together. God even cares for these little things, too. Judy and Katrina became inseparable; like Pastor Randolph mentored me Katrina did the same for Judy.

# CHAPTER 7

# Tested

Between Mama's fellowship and Grace Community Hall, I spent a lot of time learning about Jesus. The Bible became more than a good book. It became my lifeline, filled with wisdom and the truth I was looking for. At the end of February, I was to speak at a Believers Conference that was being held in the Town Hall.

It had snowed the night before the meeting yet the news was getting out how God was healing and setting people free in the meetings, and the place was packed. Mark and Judy were always by my side helping with the sound equipment, seating, and meeting the guests.

Katrina was there today. She had arrived early to pray for the meeting. I felt uneasiness in my spirit as we began to pray. I put my armor on according to Ephesians chapter 6. It's funny when I first heard this scripture, it sounded crazy and it made no sense. Today though, I know why it is very important to do this by faith. Even with this, I still had uneasiness inside my heart that I couldn't quite put my finger on. "Lord, I don't know what it is. Why do I feel this way?"

I pressed in and waited.

"Lord, I will cancel this meeting if that is what you want."

I waited. A knock came at the door. "Pastor Randolph, I am glad to see you."

"What's going on, Clint. You look worried?"

"I don't know. I can't put my finger on it, but I feel like I'm about to enter a battle."

"You are, Clint. The devil does not want this truth out. You can bet he will try something. Do you have your armor on?"

"You bet I do, according to Ephesians Chapter 6! But," I paused. "I am not going out there unless Jesus tells me to, either!"

"Okay, let's pray."

We stayed there and prayed through all the announcements, and through half of the worship. Then it happened, I could feel His sweet presence in the room. Wave after wave of His love washed over me. Then He spoke, "Matthew 10:28."

I got my Bible and turned to it. This verse read, *"And do not fear those who kill the body but cannot kill the soul. But rather fear Him who is able to destroy both soul and body in hell."*

"Wow. Okay, Lord, I will fear only You."

Then I heard, "Go."

I told Pastor Randolph, "I'm ready."

We walked out.

Pastor Randolph took a seat next to Mark, and the ladies and I sat on the stage area up front. Soon the host introduced me and I walked to the microphone . I turned my Bible to Ephesians 2:8, 9, *"For by grace you have been saved through faith, and that not of yourselves; it is the gift of God, not of works, lest anyone should boast."*

"I want to talk about this grace, a grace that would take hold of the hand of the lowest of sinners to the highest of kings, and show His Love to them. And pour His mercy on them. This is the grace that God showed me."

I glanced out at those in the crowd. They looked up at me in expectation. "I worked at a very successful pediatric office. My colleagues and I decided to close it down to open a women's clinic, because that was where the money was. I had performed an abortion where the baby was born alive. She yawned, opened her eyes, grabbed my finger, and died.–"

"Murderer!" A woman yelled.

"Why are we listening to him?" Another woman screamed.

Then the whole place erupted, some saying, "Be quiet! He's a good man!" Punches started flying. People dived across chairs. I heard yells. News reporters were there and the cameras were flashing.

Mark and Pastor Randolph were holding people back.

"People!" I called out. "Let's calm down. Let's—"

A man punched me, knocking me to the floor. Mark grabbed him, and I did my best to pull myself up. I could hardly see because of the blood in my eye and how stunned I was after I was hit.

"Pastor Randolph," I yelled, "get the girls out of here and we will meet up with you later!"

A police officer quickly took Mark and me out the back

door. By then the police were coming up from all directions! News cameras were on us. The officers snatched open my car door. Mark and I jumped in and drove away.

"Praise God, we are safe," Mark said. "Now, to meet up with the others at church."

By that time my eye was swollen shut, and the blood from the cut was nearly dry. When we got to the church, Katrina was there with her mama, who, of course, took care of me immediately.

"Lord, Clint, you just come right over here. It's going to be all right. I came over as soon as Katrina called me."

"Thank you, I'm fine," I said, trying to see out of the swollen eye.

"He's fine ... he's fine ... I can see that he's *not* fine! Clint, sit down and let me look at you," Katrina's mama said.

"Are you dizzy?" Katrina asked.

"No, I'm fine." Mama began to dab at my eye. "Ouch!"

"'Fine,' he says. You are going to need some stitches over this eye," she said.

"Ouch!" Mama dabbed it again with some peroxide.

"What happened, Clint?" Mama put down her swabbing cloth.

"I'll tell you what happened," Mark spoke up. "I noticed that after most of the people came in for the service, there was a group of five or six people ... and some reporters that came in, too. They spread out and sat in different spots of the room."

"You mean, spies?" Pastor Randolph walked over and sat down.

Mark looked at him. "That's what it looked like!"

"But who would send spies, and what did it prove?" Pastor Randolph said.

At that point, Katrina sat next to me holding an ice pack she made up. She gently held it on my eye. I moved and she said, "Be still, Clint. You were lucky that this is all that happened to you!"

I rather enjoyed her fussing over me. She was gentle and smelled like honeysuckle.

Mark finished, "When Clint was talking, one of them jumped up and shouted 'Murderer'! Another one shouted something else out, and then the crowd got into it. It was all planned; you mark my words. Thank God the police got there when they did. I thought the crowd was going to pull you apart!"

At that point, for a brief moment I didn't hear another word. I was lost in the attention that Katrina was showing me. And her sweet smell and gentle touch was somehow more comforting to me than anything anyone could say or do at that moment.

"Clint? Clint! Are you all right?"

I was brought back to the present with Pastor Randolph asking me if I was okay.

"Why don't you stay with us tonight and then go home. We would love some extra company," Pastor Randolph said.

I agreed, and we all joined hands and prayed, giving God the glory to have suffered for His name. God is so worthy! God is so worthy! Amen. That night I spoke with Pastor Randolph about the last encounter with Bill. We all sat in front of the fireplace. The crackle and pop of the burning wood was somehow comforting.

I spoke up. "Pastor Randolph, my heart is heavy about something that Bill said the last time we were together."

"What's on your heart?"

"The last time Bill and I spoke, he said that my condo and my car were bought with the money of the abortions we had performed, I was so mad and hurt at the same time that I didn't know what to do."

"Was it?"

"Yes, sad enough, it was. That's why I wanted to talk to you," I leaned forward in my seat. "In fact, everything I have was bought that way. The more I think about it, the more I want to get rid of everything!"

"What?" This time Mrs. Randolph piped in.

"Where would you live, Clint?"

"I want to give away everything! I will get another place to live and another car to drive; when my adopted father died

63

he set me up a small trust fund. It's not much. I never even touched it. By the time he died, I was with the pediatrician's practice and didn't need it, so it just sat there."

"What will you do with the money you get from the sale?"

"Give it away, to clinics around the area. What do you think?"

Pastor Randolph scratched his head. "This is awful radical. You think you're going to make it all right, giving everything away?"

"I know it sounds crazy but I bought this stuff with blood money, and I can't live with that anymore. Yes, I'm sure."

"Well I know of a warm room you can stay in when you sell your place."

I chuckled. "I just might take you up on that offer."

We sat there in silence for a while enjoying the fire, watching the flames dance around.

The next morning I was welcomed in the kitchen by the smiles of Pastor Randolph and his wife, Nan. She had made a wonderful breakfast of bacon and eggs, biscuits, and smothered potatoes. We sat around the table and talked about the Scriptures. Pastor Randolph said, "Now, you be careful when you are out and about. Now that your face is all over the papers, you don't know what people will do."

I chuckled, "I'm not afraid, but I will be more alert than before."

I rubbed my sore eye, which now had a lovely shiner on it. Nan had the sweetest voice and she was very motherly. "It looks like the swelling has gone down. That's a good sign your eye is not damaged."

"What are you going to do when you leave here?" Pastor Randolph looked a little worried.

"Go home, I guess. I've got to get caught up on some bills. I never really had to think about that before while I was working. But since I've left I've had to scale down a bit."

I smiled. "But it has been worth it in order to spend some time with the Lord. Today I need God's instruction... Where is Mark?"

"He had to go to work early today. He told me to tell you

he will call you later."

"Great, I look forward to his call. Judy sure cares for him."

"I know, and she is a great girl, too," Pastor Randolph said.

"Well, I must be going. Thank you, Pastor, for everything. I will be in touch."

With that, I was on my way. When I arrived home, there was a notice on my door to appear in court. I knew this was coming, but I still couldn't believe it. I played my answering machine: "Hello, Dr. Clint, this is Judy. Call me as soon as you get this message. Got to go. Bye."

Beep. "Clint, this is Isaiah. What is going on down there? I saw the news and heard about what happened. Call me."

Beep. "Watch your back!"

Beep. "Dr. Clint, this is Katrina. I was just checking on you. I have been praying for you. Call me back, okay?"

I called Judy back first. "Women's Clinic; this is Judy."

"Judy, what's up?"

"Dr. Clint, I'm glad you called. It was Dr. Ted."

"What are you talking about?"

She lowered her voice. "I overheard him saying to Dr. Bill that he sent a welcoming party to your meeting yesterday, and to watch for the fireworks on the news. Look, I've got to go; I'll call you later."

I hung up the phone. I knew Ted said he was going to get me back, but I had no idea he would stoop so low. Wow.

I called Katrina. "Hello?"

"Katrina, it was Ted; he set me up yesterday."

"You're kidding! I didn't think he would do something like that."

"Neither did I, but he did say he wanted to kill my reputation."

"Clint, what the devil meant for evil, God will turn around for good. Don't quit!"

"I'm not going to quit, but maybe I need to take a break for a little while." I chuckled, and she laughed, too.

I enjoyed her laughter. It was refreshing in light of everything that was gone on. "Well, I won't keep you, I'll let—"

I cut her off. "Katrina," I paused and felt somewhat embarrassed, "would you like to go to dinner tonight? I know this is short notice, but I thought I—"

She cut *me* off. "I'd love to."

"Great, I'll pick you up at 6:30. It's a date. I will see you tonight, then."

She giggled, "Yes."

"Okay, then. Bye."

"Bye."

I hung up the phone feeling like a schoolboy going on his first date. "What's wrong with me? This is crazy!"

I shook off the feeling and picked up the phone to call Isaiah. The phone rang, "Come on Isaiah, pick up the phone." It rang again and again.

I was just about to hang up when at last I heard, "Hello?"

"Isaiah, this is Clint."

"Clint! What in the world is going on down there? I saw you on the news."

"Isaiah, it's a long story! I'll meet up with you in three months. We can talk then."

"Sure Clint, I'll see you then, and try not to get into any more fights, okay?" He laughed.

"I will call you when I'm in town."

"I'll be at the Sherrington Suites," Isaiah said.

"All right. See you then."

I hung up the phone, knowing that Isaiah could make sense of everything that had been going on, and also give me some sound advice.

I looked at the time. It was already 3:30. My heart yearned to be with Jesus, so I turned off the phones and knelt down by the sofa and prayed: "Oh Lord, You have given me the very breath that I breathe. My heart belongs to you. Lord, show me Your great love because my heart is yearning for You. Teach me Your ways and let me understand Your Word, for Your Word is Truth.

"Lord, you have seen Ted's wicked acts. Lord, forgive him, for if he only knew Your intense love for him he would change. Turn his bitterness, oh God, and reveal the truth ... for he is lost without You ... like I was lost without You. Give me wisdom concerning the court case. Give me favor, oh Lord, and turn Your light on the dark areas and make everything known."

I must have been there for some time because before I knew it, it was 5. I jumped up and got ready for my date. I was a sight to be seen: one black shiner and a Band-Aid over my eye. I settled for my black turtleneck shirt and a sports jacket. I looked in the mirror and changed my shirt. I rebuked myself again, "This is ridiculous! What is my problem?"

I put the turtleneck back on. By that time it was 5:45.

Katrina lived across town, and I don't want to be late. I rolled up to her door and I was taken aback for a moment: I had looked at Katrina before, but that was the first time I was taken aback by her beauty. She had on a cream lace dress, nothing revealing, just stunning. She had her hair up with strands of it down... brushing her shoulders. I could feel my face turn red. I could hardly talk; in fact, I stumbled over my words. Mama watched as we drove off.

"So," she opened up, "where are we going tonight?"

"It's a surprise. But I know how much you like seafood."

She looked surprised. "How do you know?"

I winked. "I have my sources."

"Oh, you do?" I could hear the amusement in her voice.

"Yes, I do! I can't tell all my secrets, now can I?" I cast a quick glance at her as I turned onto the next street. "I wanted to say 'thank you' for treating my eye."

"Mama did most of the work." She smiled.

"Ah yes, but you held the ice pack."

She laughed, "And on a moving object, as I recall."

"It hurt."

"You were not a good patient."

"Thank you, doctor." We laughed.

Soon we pulled up to the Captain's Bell, a top-notch restaurant. "Clint, I can't believe it! It takes weeks to get in to eat here — how, when?"

"I've got my contacts. They treat me good here."

We were greeted as we entered, and our table was a window seat overlooking the bay. I ordered a soda water with lemon, and she ordered an ice tea. The candlelight danced on her brown skin; she seemed to glisten. This time she caught me staring at her. She blushed. I blushed. I whispered a little prayer, "Lord, why am I acting like this? It's not like I have never been out with Katrina before."

Then the Lord whispered back. "This is your wife, but you can't tell her yet. You must wait a little longer."

My expression must have been seen on my face because she asked me, "What?"

I was speechless for a moment. "Dr. Clint," she interrupted, "Clint. Clint, are you okay? You look as if you wanted to say something."

"No. I, I, I'm okay."

She smiled. I almost gave myself away. I couldn't help but look at her. She was just so beautiful. I was only rescued when our waitress came by to take our order. We ordered the smoked salmon and wild rice, shrimp in a creamy mustard sauce, and a spinach salad. The evening seemed to go by quickly as we talked about the Lord, and of His ability to unearth attitudes of the heart.

"Dinner was delicious," she said with a smile.

The waitress came back with a tray of desserts. We shared a chocolate cheesecake. She excused herself to go to the ladies room, while I sat and waited.

Then I saw Bill, sitting over in the corner of the room ... alone. I got up and walked over to him.

"Bill," I said with a smile.

Bill smiled and extended his hand. He looked happy to see me. Then his smile dropped and he pulled his hand back. "Clint."

He stood up, paid the bill, and walked out. I followed and stopped him, "Bill, no matter what happens, I'm still your friend."

My words seemed to shake him up. He looked down and left. I returned to my table, where Katrina was waiting.

"Is everything all right, Clint? Who was that you were talking to?"

"Bill."

"He seemed to be in a hurry."

"Yeah, thanks to me."

"What do you mean?"

"Let's go."

I paid the check and we strolled down the boardwalk. It was a little cool, so I gave Katrina my jacket. "Bill and Ted are both taking me to court."

"On what charges?"

"Embezzlement." The word sounded flat, even to my own ears.

"Embezzlement? They can't really hold you on this, or can they?"

"Many people have gone to jail innocent, you know." I truly did not know what would happen.

"And I'll bring you a cake with a file in it, too."

"Very funny!" We stood there looking out at the water. It was beautiful. She was beautiful. Everything inside me wanted to hold her close to me, but I would honor her and the Word of the Lord to wait.

We walked back to the car. I drove Katrina home and walked her to the door. I know that this is the part where the man gives his date a goodnight kiss. Instead, I took hold of Katrina's hand, and looking her in the eyes, I gently kissed it. She blushed.

"Thank you for a wonderful night, Clint."

"No, the pleasure was mine.

In the upcoming months Katrina and I spent more time together. I looked at her and said: "Katrina, you are a remarkable woman. Though we come from such different worlds we are held together by God's invisible bond."

She smiled and took a sip of water from a bottle she was holding. "I love hiking," she said. "After you told me there were only deer in the park and no bears, I was fine."

"I have to admit that I am still a little sore from the horseback ride and that was two days ago,"

We stopped to look off the "mountain" as she put it and down into the valley below to drink in the beauty of the scene.

Katrina spoke openly.

"I have never been around anything like this before," she confessed. "To tell the truth, the restaurant is all I've ever known."

We sat down on a large rock that overlooked the valley. I listened.

"In fact I would daydream of going places."

I piped in, "Really? Like what places?"

"Paris is one place I would love to visit, to see the Eiffel Tower and to see the French waiters. Or maybe the Leaning Tower of Pisa in Italy. Or silly as it sounds, Washington, D.C. And all the museums, the Washington Monument and the Capital. Mama was always busy running the restaurant that we never did go anywhere." She regained herself. "So where have you been?"

I opened up and shared things about me that no one knew but God. And I needed to be able to have someone know me from childhood to glory. It felt good to trust again.

We had plenty of time then to talk. I listened intensely to every word. I didn't want to miss anything about her life.

She shared: "Mama was a single parent and her mom was a single parent. Her dad left her and her younger brothers. I asked her why and she said he wanted his freedom. So she helped her mama raise her brothers plus work at the restaurant, and now we all help her."

Her face changed to a sad but serious expression. "That's why when I got pregnant I knew that Mama would be so disappointed in me and that she couldn't afford another mouth to feed, so I went and got an abortion and never told her."

Then she stopped and looked at me.

"What?" I asked.

"Why do you want to be around me?" she asked.

"Why do I want to be around you?"

She struggled a little as she asked the question, "What makes a handsome white doctor want to be with a black waitress?"

I didn't miss a beat: "Because I love chocolate!"

She laughed. "No really."

I looked her straight in the eyes. "Because you're sweet and strong and you love Jesus with all your heart and I love that." I smiled. "Besides you being beautiful," I took hold of her hand, gently kissed it, "I haven't quite mastered the art of biscuit making,"

She laughed. "That's going to take a long while!"

•

We also spent time biking and having picnics with Judy and Mark.

It was May before I knew it, and I had plans to meet with Isaiah in Maine. I waited until the last minute to tell Katrina.

"I will be leaving tomorrow to go to Maine."

"Tomorrow? But why Maine? It's, it's so far."

She sounded so cute when she said that. I smiled. "I have a dear friend — you might have heard me mention him a while back. Isaiah?"

"Yes, I have heard you speak of him." She nodded.

"Well, he has a conference there. And I promised I would come."

"When will you come back? You know the news media won't have anything to talk about while you're gone."

"Very funny!"

She looked down. I gently raised her chin. "Hey, smile. I promise I will call."

She smiled this unforgettable smile. I got into my car and drove away thinking of the last few days together and also of the opportunity that I had to speak to Bill a while back.

# CHAPTER 8

# The Dream

Iarrived early at the airport to check in. I always pack light and only had two bags with me. I sat down in the waiting area and thought about last night, when behind me I heard, "Excuse me sir, I believe you forgot something."

I turned around to see Katrina holding the jacket that I let her wear the night we walked on the boardwalk.

"Katrina!" I jumped up ... I laughed. "What are you doing here?"

"You forgot your jacket and I, ah, thought you, ah, might need it. Anyway, you didn't even see me coming. It seems like you were miles away."

"Not miles away. You caught me thinking about how we met and how my life has changed because of it."

She blushed. "To tell you the truth, that's why I came. I couldn't stop thinking about everything you did, all the fun we had yesterday and," she paused, "I got to missing you."

I sat there just looking at her. She had her hair down and she wore a red and white baseball shirt.

"Um-m-m, you didn't say when you were coming back." She said with a pout.

"My plane should land on the 20th."

"A week! What am I going to do for a week? I had my ice pack all ready."

"Very funny." I stared at her for a moment; neither of us was talking. "Flight 280 now boarding at gate 12. Flight 280 now boarding at gate 12."

"Well! That's my plane."

I took hold of Katrina's hand and kissed it again. "Thank you."

"For what?"

"For bringing me my jacket."

"My pleasure."

"Last call for flight 280. Now boarding at gate 12."

"You had better go; they are about to close the door!" Then she smiled this incredible smile that lit my whole heart up. "See you soon!"

Aboard the plane, I took my seat in first class next to the window. As we taxied down the runway, I could feel a longing to be back again and I hadn't even left yet! Before I knew it the seat belt sign was off and we were airborne. My thoughts returned to the airport and to Katrina. I could not seem to get her out of my thoughts. I could still smell her perfume on my jacket and her smile was etched on my heart.

"Lord, how am I going to wait when I feel like this? Lord, I give Katrina to you; she belongs to you and not to me. Forgive me, Lord, for taking that which you have not given to me yet. Amen."

I turned my thoughts toward Isaiah. I had so much to tell him, I didn't know where to start. "Lord, will you please talk to Isaiah, too?"

I drifted off to sleep and dreamed I was back at the clinic again. Judy was there and she greeted me with a smile. I went into my office. It had become Ted's office. It had his pictures of his family on the desk. I picked up his coat and put it on, thinking that it was mine. I went in to perform an abortion, but the girl was Ted's wife. I backed up in surprise.

She said, "You're not touching me, you Embezzler!"

I looked down and in his coat pocket was a bank deposit slip with all this money stuck to it. Judy's face changed and it wasn't her anymore. She started chanting, "Embezzler! Embezzler!"

Ted appeared, laughing and pulling money out of the coat pocket that I was wearing. The picture began to get distorted. They all backed me into a corner, chanting "Embezzler," while Ted just stood there ... laughing this wicked laugh.

"No. No." I tossed and turned my head, "No."

"Sir? Sir? Wake up, you are having a dream."

I woke with a jump.

"Are you okay?"

It was the steward; he looked concerned.

"You were dreaming."

Sweat was coming down my face. Boy was I glad to be out of that dream! The seat belt sign came on, and the captain informed us that we would arrive shortly. I was glad, too. Once we landed, I called Judy and told her to check the pockets of the jackets hanging in our office. She said she would do her best. I called Isaiah, "Hello?"

"Isaiah, this is Clint. My plane just landed."

"Great! I can't wait to see you!"

After I got my luggage, I stood outside looking for Isaiah. He was standing over by a cab, waving to me. "Boy, are you a sight for sore eyes. It is good to see you," I said.

"And I am glad to see you, my friend. Now tell me what is going on?"

"You bet I will. The news media has had a feeding frenzy."

"Well, you can tell me about it at the hotel."

I checked into a business suite. There was plenty of room and a whole conference table to boot. We sat down.

"Do you remember the little waitress at the restaurant when you were down last?"

"Yes, yes. I think I remember her. A pretty little thing. She gave you her phone number, right?"

"Right."

"Ah, Clint, you sly fox; you called her, huh? You lucky fellow!"

"It was not like that at all. We went out a couple of times then one of those times I had heard the Voice again, I was forced then to talk about what had been happening to me." I chuckled, "I thought she would jump up and walk out thinking I was crazy but she didn't."

Isaiah nodded. "Go on."

"She shared with me the same Scripture that you pointed out."

"Remarkable."

"What was truly remarkable was what happened next."

"What happened, Clint?"

"She shared that this Voice had a name, Jesus, and that He was trying to get my attention because I was killing His creation. My heart began to break. We knelt down right there in the park, and I asked for God's forgiveness. Isaiah, I could see a book."

"A book? What kind of a book?"

"A book that had every abortion that I had ever performed.

It also had the name of every girl I had been with, and every time I had scorned a Christian. Man, I tell you, Isaiah, it had everything that I had ever done in my life. Nothing was left out!"

"Clint, what you're saying is impossible! It sounds insane!"

"I know it does, but you know me better than that! You yourself found the same verse in the Bible after I told you about the 'Voice'."

Isaiah got up and began to walk around. "What happened next, after you saw this ..." he paused, "... this book?"

"Well, I fell to my knees and knew that I was guilty. I began to repent for everything item by item, as it was shown to me. I cried like a baby as I was shown the bloody past of each sin that I had committed."

"And did He forgive you?"

"As I repented, each page was wiped clean until I heard, 'Peace. Now, all is done.' I prayed and received Jesus Christ into my heart and life. I have said I will go and do whatever He wants. After that happened, I no longer could perform abortions, so I quit."

Isaiah's eyes widened. "You quit?"

"Yes, I quit! I no longer wanted the blood of the unborn on my hands."

Isaiah waited for me to continue.

"Well, you can only guess Bill and Ted's reaction. Ted hit the fan, and told me he was going to ruin me. The next thing I know, the media is knocking at my door asking questions about embezzling."

"Embezzling? That's impossible! I don't like it."

"Like what?"

"Embezzlement. Why did he say 'embezzling'? It strikes me funny that he would use those words."

"What are you saying, Isaiah?"

"Why didn't he use words like: Partnership or breaking a contract? Why embezzling?"

"I did have this dream in the plane on the way here. I won't go into the whole dream, but in one part, I reached into the pocket of my office coat and found out that I had put on Ted's coat instead. Inside was a bank deposit slip for a Swiss account. It had money stuck to it."

"Are you thinking what I am thinking, Clint?"

"I already called Judy and asked her to check the pockets of the coats in our office."

"When is your court case?"

"Wednesday July the 25th. At 9."

"That's in a couple of months, Clint! What are you doing here?"

"I needed to talk with you. So much has happened to me that I needed a true friend."

"Thank you. Now, do you have a good lawyer?"

I shook my head. "Not yet."

"I know of a good one. His name is Michael Bonovitch. As a matter of fact, he's up here at the convention. I will introduce him to you."

"Great! I knew I could count on you. Isaiah, you're the best."

"You just get out of this mess and that will be thanks enough!"

"Isaiah, Jesus is real and He is the Messiah. I know, Isaiah! I heard His voice."

"Clint, I know that's what you told me, but He hasn't spoken to me yet! And I have studied every book out there and, nothing! He must prove Himself to me in order for me to believe! Look, I must go and rest up for tonight. We can talk about this later, okay?"

I nodded and Isaiah left.

I wondered what lay ahead.

# CHAPTER 9

# Forgiveness

Two hours later, the phone rang. It was Isaiah.

"Clint, you've got to come over. Hurry, Clint. I need to talk to you!"

He sounded desperate, so I rushed down to his room.

"Clint, you will never believe what has happened to me."

He had hold of my shirt and I gently took his hand off. "Come on, Isaiah, sit down and tell me what's going on."

"Okay."

He sat.

"When I came back to my room, I laid down to rest up for tonight's meeting."

"Okay. Go on."

"I had a dream. Verse after verse and scripture after scripture came to me!"

"What are you talking about?"

"The Bible! Scriptures that talk about the Messiah!"

Tears were flowing down his face. I had never seen him like this before. "I have searched all my life and read everything I could in pursuit of the Messiah and now, Clint, I have found him! What do I do now? I am not worthy of such a great honor."

"Let's kneel down, Isaiah, and ask God for forgiveness."

"I don't know where to start," he said.

"Just start at what He shows you first, and then go down the list."

"Oh Jesus, I have mocked You and those You have sent my way. Will You please forgive me? I have loved the praise of men and the power that I felt as I held their attention."

Between the repentance of sin and the outward sobs that would well up from deep down, Isaiah was converted. Oh, the rejoicing that came from that room at that moment. Could it be true or was this a dream? To have my friend, father, and now my brother truly converted to Christ! If it were a dream, it is one that I did not want to wake up from!

Then reality set in, and Isaiah stood still and said. "Clint, what shall I say at the meeting tonight? It is in only an hour?"

"Ask Him."

"Is it that simple? Just ask Him?"

"Yes. It is that simple."

Isaiah looked nervous. "Okay, I will! ... Jesus, what is it you want me to speak tonight before these people?"

Just then it was as if a light went off inside of Isaiah's head.

"What is it?" I asked.

"Luke 12, verse 11 and 12.

"That's in the New Testament, Clint." He got the Bible out of the night table and held it up.

"I used to throw these in the trash. I never thought I would be holding one close to my heart."

He opened the Bible and turned to the verse. *"Now when they bring you to the synagogues and magistrates and authorities, do not worry about how or what you should answer, or what you should say. For the Holy Spirit will teach you in that very hour what you ought to say."*

Then we broke out into this wonderful laughter to know we don't have to worry about anything. This was freedom. "I've got to go get ready. I will meet you downstairs."

We took a cab. "I was offered a limo, but I'd rather not be noticed when I come to the Convention Hall," Isaiah said.

When we arrived there was limo after limo parked out front. Inside, it was packed. There were tables with books and CDs and DVDs that Isaiah had written, and other tables as well, all along the walls. There were people who came up to Isaiah and greeted him after they realized he was there. I knew Isaiah was important but, wow, I just took a step back. There were all types of dignitaries, as well as rabbis and other Jewish leaders and teachers. There were those from other faiths, including Buddhists, Hindus, and well-known Christian leaders.

Inside the auditorium I don't believe there was an empty seat. Well, maybe one — mine — up front toward the right. Isaiah walked up on the stage.

This time he looked a little nervous.

And then God gave me the Scripture verse Luke 12:8: *"Also I say to you, whoever confesses Me before men, him the Son of*

*Man also will confess before the angels of God."*

I quickly wrote it down on a note pad and gave it to Isaiah. He read it and gained confidence.

After a long introduction, Isaiah took the floor. My heart pounded inside. It was kind of like waiting for the other shoe to drop. I felt uneasy, like something was going to happen. "Friends, scholars, and those who have journeyed here from so far, I welcome you."

The crowd erupted with applause, and then fell silent again.

"*'In the beginning, God ...'* The depth of that beginning can reach across the billions and billions of years that have come and gone. And yet we, as humans, had no idea what this simple phrase could mean. Think about the drop of water that comes from dew, rain or river; we don't even care about that single tiny drop. It simply is there and then gone, along with all of its life-giving force. Now, why would a God who holds galaxies in the palm of His hand even care about that one single drop of water? Or why should He care about that one single grain of sand? Or why should He care about you or me? *'In the beginning, God.'* He knew us, each strand of DNA. You might ask, 'Why should that matter? Why is the DNA of mankind so important?' Are we not like that tiny drop of water? Here for a moment and then vanished away?'"

Isaiah went on holding our attention like a fine craftsman or an ironworker with his anvil. "Many of you have read the books that I have written and you've sat in on many of my debates. You have seen me in the news; in magazines and other literature and you know that I, too, am in search for the truth. I have read every Holy Book out there and debated with the best of scholars. Still, I didn't know for sure about this God, who was in the beginning and is now alive and real."

I could hear the audience stirring and talking. "Today, my friends, I have met this God. I lay upon my bed to rest before coming here. While I was sleeping, these Scriptures came to my eyes:

'Isaiah 53:1-5, *"Who has believed our report? And to whom*

*has the arm of the LORD been revealed? For He shall grow up before Him as a tender plant, and as a root out of dry ground. He has neither form nor comeliness; and when we see Him, there is no beauty that we should desire Him. He is despised and rejected by men, a Man of sorrows, and acquainted with grief. And we hid, as it were, our faces from Him; He was despised, and we did not esteem Him. Surely he has borne our grief and carried our sorrows; yet we esteemed Him stricken, smitten by God, and afflicted. But He was wounded for our transgressions, He was bruised for our iniquities; the chastisement for our peace was upon Him, and by His stripes we are healed."*

Isaiah 26:19, *"Your dead shall live; together with my dead body they shall arise. Awake and sing, you who dwell in dust; for your dew is like the dew of herbs, and the earth shall cast out the dead."*

Psalm 16:10 reads, *"For You will not leave my soul in Sheol, nor will You allow Your Holy One to see corruption."*

Jeremiah 31:3, *"The LORD has appeared of old to me, saying: Yes, I have loved you with an everlasting love; therefore with loving kindness I have drawn you."*

"These Scriptures kept appearing before my eyes, and when I woke up," he paused, "I heard with my own ears, 'I am Jesus and I am the Messiah!'"

That was it: The other shoe had finally dropped. It was like something out of a movie. Someone stood up and shouted, "Blasphemy!"

The crowd went crazy: Throwing paper and books in the air, putting their hands over their ears, and shouting one thing, then another. Security came rushing in; the news reporters were having a field day. People jumped up and left and Isaiah was trying to get everyone's attention, which was not working.

Then something amazing happened. A crowd of people, some old, but mostly young men and women began to gather at the stage area. They had tears running down their faces. They began to say,

"What shall we do?"

I beckoned for Isaiah to come over to them, which he did.

"Tell us what shall we do? We know what you say is truth."

"Repent of your sins. Name each one and then invite Jesus the Messiah to take over the ownership of your life."

Their eyes were glued to him. "Will you help us, Isaiah?"

"Yes will you help us? Buddha has never made my heart ache inside like this. I must have Jesus!"

I thought I was Christian all these years but I have never given over total control to Jesus! I want my life to change!"

"Yes. Yes. Let us kneel down right here," he beckoned for me to come closer. "My friend here will also help."

So there in the midst of the craziness — the security escorting people out and the news reporters scrambling to record the chaos — God came down. And for that moment, time seemed to have stopped.

"I will come back tonight for part two of the seminar; so come back then."

With lots of hugs and tears, everyone was dismissed.

"Tonight? Isaiah, do you think they will let you come back tonight?"

Isaiah laughed. "It's already paid for."

When we came back later, there were only a handful of people. The book tables in the lobby were empty, but that is not what they came for. The people came hungry for more of the truth. They came hungry to hear more about the Messiah, and Isaiah was ready. Amid the group was a dignitary from Ethiopia and a Jewish rabbi. The small number of people didn't seem to have an effect on Isaiah. In fact, he seemed a little relieved. What were 50 or 60 people versus the hundreds he had this afternoon? This time Isaiah asked me if I would speak to the people, too. I was honored.

Later that night Isaiah kept me awake, asking me question after question as scripture after scripture came to life. I told him everything I knew and we prayed and he sang a song. "All my life I have searched for Messiah ... all my life until I met Jesus, who is the Messiah. Clint, I feel like a child."

"That's great, Isaiah, but I am tired and I have a plane to

catch in the morning."

"Oh, of course, my friend. I'm sorry, but there is so much to learn."

"It all starts with the Word of God: Pick it up and learn it all over again, but this time with the Messiah leading you. Pray and think on what you read and I'll be in touch later on. I'll be talking to Michael Bonovitch when I get back."

"That's right! Is there anything else I can do, Clint?"

"No. It's enough to know that my friend and mentor knows Jesus the Messiah."

"Then I will pray for you, Clint."

Back at the airport I sat and had time to think. My plane did not leave for another hour. I chuckled to myself, "Maybe I should write a book." I had been looking out the window and hadn't even noticed a young man in his twenties sitting across from me.

"Excuse me? Aren't you the doctor from the convention?"

I smiled and said, "That depends, if that's a good thing."

He smiled. "It's a good thing. I gave my life over to Yeshua after Dr. Isaiah spoke. He spoke with such power! It was like something happened that moment, and I knew that this must be true. My heart was burning inside. Every part of me could feel Messiah's touch. I could hear Messiah's voice speaking to me, and I wanted Him more than life itself!"

"Are you up here alone?"

"I came up with my roommate, but after he saw what happened at the meeting," he looked down, "he caught a plane and went home."

"What's your name?"

"Aaron. Aaron Cohen."

"Well, Aaron would you like a travel partner?"

"Would I!" His smile was contagious. He wasn't very tall, but he was strong. I could see that he lifted weights. His shirtsleeve was tight against his arm, making my arm look skinny in comparison. His hair was short and had that wavy look to it. He wore a small blue cap on top of his head like Isaiah. He was full of questions, and I was happy to answer any that he had. Little did I know then that Aaron would later grow to be my "Timothy" — a young man I would mentor, just as Paul mentored Timothy. Praise be to God! Until then I had a hungry baby bird on my hands.

He told me where he was from, and I chuckled. I have driven by that college plenty of times. We exchanged information and I told him about Mama's Place and Pastor Randolph. Time seemed to have stopped as we talked about Jesus. It wasn't long before the plane was landing.

Katrina greeted me. She was waiting for me at the end of the ramp. I was so happy to see her. "Aaron, this is Katrina."

"Glad to meet you," she said with a broad smile. "So, how do you know Clint?"

"I was at a convention given by Dr. Isaiah."

"How was the convention?"

"I met the Messiah there."

Her smile grew wider, if possible. "That's wonderful!"

I greeted her with a hug. "You are a sight for sore eyes! I've got to get one more bag and I'll be ready. How did you know I was coming back today?"

"You told me."

"I did? Hmm. Well, I'm glad I did."

"We are having a special meeting tonight to pray for you and the court case."

Aaron looked concerned. "Court case? What's that all about?"

"It's a long story, but I will try to make it short. After I turned my life over to Jesus, I left my practice at a women's clinic."

Aaron was confused. "Is that required?"

"It is if you are an abortionist."

The confusion vanished. "Oh."

"However, my partners didn't think that was a good idea and are taking me to court. One of them is trying to sue me for embezzlement. He swears that he will ruin my name. So, there it is in a nutshell."

Katrina stepped in, "And that's why we want to pray for him tonight. So will you be there? Aaron, you are invited, too."

He paused for a second and said, "I would love to come. Of course I will be there."

"Aaron, meet us at the address I gave you for Mama's Place."

We both embraced Aaron and then got into the car.

"How is Isaiah?"

"Isaiah is fine. He knows the Lord now."

She looked at me with wonderment, waiting for me to continue.

I smiled and went on, "You won't believe this, but after a failed attempt to share Jesus with him, he called me on the phone two hours later."

"Really?"

"He sounded frantic, so I hurried down to his room." I chuckled to myself. "He looked freaked out and grabbed my shirt, telling me that Scripture after Scripture kept appearing to him. All of them were speaking about the Messiah."

"Wow!"

"You're not kidding, 'Wow!' He said that Jesus spoke to him and told him that He was the Messiah."

"That's incredible."

"We knelt down and prayed."

"That's wonderful!" Katrina clapped.

"Well, he had to put his faith into practice right away."

"What do you mean?"

"He had a meeting that night, and not just any meeting either. There were important people there: Rabbis, scholars from different countries and Jews, Christians and Buddhists. There were limos pulling up. To tell the truth, I was a little intimidated. Isaiah did look a little worried until the Lord gave me this Scripture — Luke 12:8, 'Also I say unto you, whosoever shall confess me before men, him shall the Son of man also confess before the angels of God'."

"Then what happened?" "Well, he jumped into it with both feet."

Katrina knew what that meant. "And let me guess, not everyone agreed with his speech?"

I shook my head, remembering the wild scene. "People

started shouting and throwing paper into the air. Security had to escort some people out the door; others left."

"But where did you get Aaron?"

"I met him at the airport. It turns out he was one of those who came to the Lord that night."

"Wait a minute! What happened?"

I paused as I relived the moment. I felt the same peace that had entered the room while we were praying at the seminar enter into the car as I shared the story with Katrina. "In all that craziness that was going on, a group of 50 or 60 people gave up ownership of their lives to Jesus."

"And Aaron is one of those believers?" I nodded my head, too choked up to speak. The rest of the drive home was in silence, surrounded by the peace of the Lord. "Thank you, Katrina, for picking me up."

She smiled, "No problem. See you tonight."

# CHAPTER 10

# Edward

Iwas glad to get home. My answering machine was blinking "Full.

Beep! "You have 28 messages."

I took off my shoes as the messages began to play. "Hello. Edward? I am praying for you. I know you haven't heard from me in years. Call me, okay? Aunt Deb."

I took a deep breath. My heart leaped inside of me. I hadn't heard anyone call me by that name in years. She sounded old, and there was a sweet yet sad sound in her voice. It was a "familiar sound," when I once knew her by a "welcoming sound." I picked up the phone and dialed the number. Why was I so nervous?

"Hello. Aunt Deb?"

"Edward, is it really you? Thank Heaven that I found you again before …"

She paused.

"Before what?"

"Oh, never mind that. How are you?"

"How did you find me? I thought that you were dead," I blurted out. "I thought I was alone."

"That's something I would like to talk about. May I see you soon?"

"I would love to see you. Where do you live?"

"In Atlanta, Georgia on Glendale Street."

"If all goes well, I will see you in two weeks."

"Edward, I need to see you before that. I am not well."

"Okay.. Sure. How about –"

She cut me off. "Tomorrow. Can you come tomorrow?"

The urgency in her tone startled me, but I didn't hesitate. "Sure, no problem."

"Oh, good," she said. Then, "Edward, I have heard the news talk about you embezzling. Is that true?"

I rubbed my hand over my eyes and forehead. "No, it's not true. I am being set up by one of the doctors I worked with. All because I became a Christian and quit the women's clinic."

"That's awful! I will pray that all that is held in secret will be shouted from the rooftops!"

"Thank you, Aunt Deb."

"Then Edward, I will see you tomorrow, right?"

"Right."

"Goodbye, Edward."

"Goodbye, Aunt Deb."

Tears were in my eyes. "God, you do all things well!"

I knew that the meeting was in three hours and I needed a good nap, so I lay down on the sofa and drifted quickly to sleep. I was dreaming, and found myself in the Women's Clinic, walking down the hallway. I passed the first set of offices, then the second set of offices; and as I walked on, I could hear babies crying. With each step, the sound grew louder and louder...as all around me grew darker and darker. As I reached out to open up the examining door, I felt like I was walking into something. It was deep all around me, and I could smell blood.

I opened the door and there was Ted waist-deep in blood. He looked at me and started laughing. He started pulling money out of the blood that surrounded us. The sound grew louder and louder. I called out to Jesus for help! Then a light came into the room. It was brighter than anything I had ever seen. The light showed the bloodstains all over me. Ted started shouting at me. Then, Jesus reached out His hand and touched me, and I was out of the clinic and back in my living room.

I woke up with a jump. I drifted off to sleep again. This time I slept very peacefully and without interruption.

My alarm went off to remind me to get ready to go to the meeting tonight. This time I got to Mama's Place early. They were setting up chairs in the back area. Mama, Pastor Randolph, and Katrina greeted me.

"So this is the 'minds behind the meetings'?"

We laughed and embraced.

"Pastor Randolph, it is good to see you. I am waiting on a young man who met the Messiah while at the convention in Maine. I want you to talk with him if you could."

"I will be glad to, Clint; that is wonderful news."

"Well, what can I do to help?"

"I'm not sure. You need to ask Katrina," Pastor Randolph said. "She keeps me pretty busy."

"Katrina, I hear that you are the one to report to for duty. How can I help?" She smiled as our eyes connected and then she blushed and looked down.

"Well, we do need the song books put out on each chair," She said.

"My pleasure."

Just then Aaron walked into the room.

"Aaron! I'm glad you could make it!" I embraced him and patted him on the back.

"There is someone I want you to meet. Pastor Randolph, I want you to meet Aaron."

Aaron reached out to shake Pastor Randolph's hand.

Pastor Randolph smiled at him warmly. "Glad to meet you. I hear you just met the Messiah?"

Aaron chirped, "Yes, I did!"

"Well, son, you are in the right place tonight."

"Look, I've got to put the rest of these songbooks out," I said. "I could use a hand." Both Pastor Randolph and Aaron grabbed some books to help.

The room began to fill up quickly. The worship began with song after song. Tears rolled down my face, as my heart felt it was going to explode with love for the Father. I looked over at Aaron and he sat there, weeping like a baby, knowing for the first time the intense love of Jesus. When worship was over, Mama took the floor. "Oh God, we glorify Your name. We magnify Your holy, holy name, Jesus. Thank you, Father. Thank you, Father. Amen. And amen."

A chorus of amens erupted as she finished praying.

"Isn't God good, folks? I just never get enough of lifting up the name of Jesus. Amen? Tonight we are going to do a couple of things. Amen? Many of you have watched the news about Dr. Clint, right? We believe that he is being set up! Amen? And that the Devil is a liar! Amen? Amen! We are going to pray for him as a group. Amen? We are going to pray that the truth be told! Amen! After we pray, we will hear from Pastor Randolph."

92

Twenty minutes later after some powerful and anointed prayer for me, Pastor Randolph took the floor. "Let us pray. Here we are, Lord, not wanting to go forward without you. Not wanting to go backward without you. Not even wanting to stand still without you. So Lord, we wait on you. Quicken the Word tonight. May it fall on hungry hearts, we ask in the holy, matchless name of Jesus. Amen."

He transitioned from prayer into the message of the evening.

"Samson, in the Old Testament, had some 'foxes.' He had areas in his life that he refused to lay down before God. These areas when–left to themselves are like foxes that come to steal. It is clearly seen in his relationship with his parents, his wife, and ultimately with God. Any area not yielded over to Jesus will become like a fox, and it will steal your walk with God.

Folks let me encourage you to read the Word of God, and to know it for yourself. If it is hard for you to understand write it down, then ask God to make it clear to you as you read it. Lay down all ownership of your life. You were bought with a price, God gave everything for you. So when you say that you have given all to Jesus search your heart. Have you? Really? What about time? When He calls you to come pray and fellowship with Him in the wee hours of the night, do you roll over until it's a better time for you? How about that brother or sister you're not talking to? Maybe it's because he or she didn't do something for you, or did something to you so now they stay locked up inside your heart and every time when something or someone reminds you of them, you take them out of your pocket and smack them around. Bitterness, unforgiveness and pride (it's not my fault) these are 'little foxes' waiting on the sidelines to snatch up the fruit that God has planted in your life."

At that point I thought my heart would beat out of my chest. I had so much to forgive, and my dad was at the top of the list. Then it was Ted and Bill. I was pegged, and I knew it! I didn't want to wait for the altar call. I was guilty and I didn't want anything to stand between Jesus and me. So I knelt down right there while he was speaking, using my chair as an altar and repented for each one. It was not easy to forgive some of those folks I've held captive for a long time, but this was right there in front of me. I knew my walk with the Lord would come to a standstill if I did not let them go.

I was not the only one who found a place on the floor in front of their chair. I could hear the weeping and the rejoicing of different ones around the room, as they worked it through with Jesus. Aaron was one of those who found himself kneeling in front of his makeshift altar.

Then Pastor Randolph said, "Don't let this moment pass you by. Make it right with God. He already knows your heart and He's waiting for you to be honest."

I thought I was down there forever! I released everyone I held tight to, and, as I lifted my hands, my heart burst into joy! I knew the work was done. It was 11 p.m. before I left the meeting. I knew I could catch a few winks of sleep on the plane, so I lingered just a little longer and talked with some of the brothers at the meeting. I found Katrina and told her briefly about my aunt and the importance of my meeting with her tomorrow. I also told Pastor Randolph the same thing as I left the meeting.

The next day, I was at the airport early, and this time I didn't tell Katrina anything about the flight details. I wanted my heart and mind to remain on Jesus. I settled in on the plane and remembered what Pastor Randolph had spoken on, and I found myself wrestling with memories of my childhood. I knew that I had given all my hurts over to God and all of my bitterness, too – but I found myself full of old memories. I picked up my Bible to read it and a note fell out. It was from Katrina and read, "Dear Clint, I find myself praying for you more and more; In fact, I find myself thinking about you more. I enjoy being with you. You make me laugh. To watch how God is growing you up so quickly is great. Clint, even though we come from such different backgrounds, we seem to understand each other. I'm not even sure why I'm even writing this letter. It's just that when I'm with you, time stands still. Smiles. Katrina."

94

If I were driving I would have turned the car around right then and there, but I guess that is why the Lord had me find this note at this time. Hum-m-m! His timing is amazing. I never thought I could love someone so sweet and kind, and thoughtful to others. She was everything I have looked for in a wife and more. Just then the "Fasten Seatbelt" sign came on. I wasn't able to nap on the plane. In fact, I no longer felt tired: I found myself with a mix of new emotions. I knew now that Katrina was interested in me as much as I was interested in her. But I knew I could not tell her how I felt just yet. I knew that she had caught me staring at her in the meeting last night, and if I were not careful my heart would betray me. "Lord, will you keep me faithful to Your request?"

I didn't pack a bag, knowing I would be coming home that evening, so I went upstairs to the exit to flag down a cab.

"Excuse me, are you Edward Peterson?" There stood a slender, well-dressed driver.

"Yes, I am."

"I am here to pick you up. Mrs. Worshell sent me. This way, please."

Outside was a limo. He opened the door and I climbed in. Wow, I had no idea that Aunt Deb was so well off. Here was a sign: Alpharetta, 5 miles. There was no conversation on the way there, and I was left to enjoy the view.

We finally pulled in front of a huge ranch-style home. I had never seen a house so beautiful! The landscaping was something out of a garden magazine: sculptured trees and hedges set in an array of flowers. Beautiful green and white Buckeyes, orange and yellow native Azaleas and pink Redbuds painted the grounds. I couldn't believe the fountain in the middle of the driveway had hand-carved goldfish. It was amazing! The railings on the steps going up had such incredible detail. It was like walking into a dream.

Well-mannered servants greeted me. They were neatly dressed, too. They took me to a study, asked if I wanted something to drink and promptly brought it to me. From the moment I arrived to the time I left I was pampered over!

About five minutes later, I was led to Aunt Deb's room.

She was in bed and very ill. Her hair was gray and pulled up in a bun, and she was thin and frail. "Aunt Deb?"

She strengthened herself. "My little Edward. You're not so little anymore, however." She chuckled.

I was at a loss for words, seeing her in such a state. "I didn't know … I."

"Sh-h-h, now! How could you? Come and sit next to me." She patted the bed.

I stumbled through my words. "I had so many questions, but now it seemed that I had forgotten them all."

"Maybe I can help." She spoke slowly, compared to the other day when we had talked to each other. "First, let me explain why I disappeared." She paused. "Your mother and I were separated after she went back to your father. You see, he would beat your mom, and she would call me and I would help her out. This happened time and time again. I told her that she needed to leave him. Well, he was fired from his job and began to become more violent."

"Yes, I do remember something happening one night; I was awakened with yelling." I stopped for a moment. I began to feel the pain of the past … feelings I had suppressed for years.

"Mom was in the dark, drinking and crying; she was…" I stopped, "beat up. Dad had left that night and you came and got us."

She gave an almost imperceptible nod. "That was before I got married."

"How come I don't remember those days?"

"Well, after things were going along okay, Matt showed up again. Before I knew it, your mom went back to him."

I could feel the tears well up.

"I didn't hear from anyone until it was too late," she said, wiping away tears of regret.

All the memories flooded back again of that horrible time. They were fighting. I was in the backyard again; that's where I would go when they started. A gunshot went off. It scared me so I hid behind a barrel out back! Dad called for me, but I didn't move. Then I heard the car drive off really fast. I slowly went inside when all was quiet.

There on the floor by the living room chair was Mom. Tears flowed down our cheeks as I re-lived the story. I bent down next to her and touched her; she was still alive. I called the police, and held her hand. She was bleeding from her side.

"Edward," she spoke softly. "Edward, tell Deb that I'm sorry. Promise me now. Kiss me, and I will see you in heaven." Her breathing was labored. "You be brave now."

I kissed her and that was it. By the time the police got there it was too late. They had to pry my hand from hers, because I didn't want to let go.

"What happened after that?" Aunt Deb wanted to know.

"I don't remember what happened after that. I went into foster care."

"Oh, my Edward. I am so sorry. Will you forgive me for not being there for you?"

"Of course I will. I was adopted by a wonderful couple named Clint."

I bent over and embraced her. "Of course I do." We both wept.

"I got married and moved away with no forwarding address." Aunt Deb's voice was muffled as I embraced her. "I just disappeared. I never guessed this would have happened."

"No one did, and I was given a new last name when I was adopted and that's why you couldn't find me. Enough with me. Now what is going on with you?" I asked, taking in her tiny frame.

"I'm dying, Edward. I've got breast cancer; there's nothing they can do. It's spread to my lungs and now to my liver."

"But there is something that God can do! They might be ready for you to die, Aunt Deb, but I just found you again", my voice cracked, "and I'm not ready to let you go just now!"

"Sh-h-h now. I'm ready and I'm tired, too. I want to see Jesus and you don't want to deny me of such a joy, now do you?" The tears streamed down my face faster. Aunt Deb reached over and dried them.

"Now, now there is a reason I wanted you to come see

me." She reached over and rang a bell; in walked one of her servants.

"Please ask Mr. Montgomery to come in."

"Mr. Montgomery?"

"He's my lawyer. I asked him to come. Edward, my husband and I had no children and neither of us had any living relatives, so I'm giving all that I have to you."

"Aunt Deb, I, I."

She gently touched my lips. "Sh-h-h. Now God would have it this way. He has answered my prayers: You are now a Christian. And I believe He will work on your behalf concerning this court case, too."

A man entered the room carrying a briefcase.

"Mr. Montgomery, this is my nephew, Dr. Edward Peterson."

"It's Edward Clint now."

We shook hands. "Glad to meet you. Your aunt has spoken a lot about you. I was concerned, however, if we would ever find you."

My heart sank. I cleared my throat. "I'm glad you did."

"Edward, he has some papers for you to sign. You can do that in the study. Thank you, Montgomery."

We headed out of the room. "I will see you after the trial, Aunt Deb."

She smiled the warmest smile. It captured every memory I had of my aunt in her sweet expression. She had such peace, and it was all over her. We embraced. Her thin little body was frail; I wept deeply.

"Sh-h-h now. We will meet again. So don't worry about a thing. Now, you've got papers to sign and a plane to catch."

"I love you, Aunt Deb." "I love you too, my Edward. Come on! Jesus has done great things!"

I nodded my head. "He has indeed."

It took everything for me to walk out that room. I met with Mr. Montgomery. After the papers were signed, he handed me a large envelope and said, "This is the paperwork on all of your aunt's estate. Everything is listed out for you, and if you have any questions at all, my number is at the top."

"Thank you."

We walked to the door. I got back into the limo and we drove off. The drive back to the airport seemed short compared to the ride there. My heart ached from the fresh memories that now flooded my mind. I was on my plane buckled in. Soon, we were in flight. I was tired and emotionally drained! I wished I could talk to Katrina right then, to hear her sweet and gentle voice. I drifted off to sleep and heard, "Now you may tell her."

Before I knew it, the "Fasten Seatbelt" sign was on and the plane was landing. I woke up and called Katrina when we received the all-clear to use cell phones. It rang. "Hello?"

"Katrina, it's Clint. Could you meet me at the airport?"

"Sure, is everything all right?"

"More than all right. We are about to get off the plane. So I'll be waiting."

By the time I got off the plane and made my way through the airport, she had arrived. Her hair was down on her shoulders, and she had on a soft pink dress. I walked up to her, looked at her eyes and her smile, and scooped her up in my arms and held her tight.

People were passing us on both sides. Then I did something I didn't plan on: I knelt down. "Katrina, God spoke to me the night we had dinner that you are to be my wife, but I couldn't say it to you yet. He wouldn't let me, but now He told me to speak. Katrina Robinson, will you marry me?"

For that moment time stood still.

"Yes! I will be honored to marry you, Dr. Edward Clint."

I stood up and the crowd around us began clapping, which brought a blush to her cheeks again. I thought my heart would explode with joy as I held her in my arms. I gave no thought of the court case to come. I only thought of the love I was now free to express.

## CHAPTER 11

# We Head to Court

B ut three weeks did pass and the day did come, and I woke early to knocking at my door. This time I peeked through the blinds to see a yard full of reporters and camera crews. I spent some time before the Lord in prayer. I headed outside, forcing my way through a sea of reporters. "Dr. Clint, is it true that you've embezzled thousands of dollars?"

"No comment!"

"Are you the leader of a cult?"

"No!"

"Isn't it true that you quit working because of your wild living?"

I got into my car and drove off with a trail of cars behind me.

I had a good lawyer who knew his stuff … a brilliant man. I knew I was in good hands. My lawyer was waiting for me in the lobby. We shook hands.

"How do you feel? Nervous?"

I answered, "A Bit."

"Well, don't be. It will show in the courtroom, so take a deep breath and relax."

"I spoke with Judy briefly about the case and that I may call on her to testify," I said.

"Do you think she is reliable?" my attorney asked.

"Judy is solid as a rock."

"Do you know anybody else who can speak on your behalf?"

"No."

"Then we will wait to call their bluff." He looked at his watch.

"It's almost time to go in … So you think that Judy has information that will help our case."

"I'm not sure of it, but I have a hunch she does."

My attorney looked skeptical. "But how can you be so certain?"

"I had a dream."

The skepticism turned to annoyance. "You what? Come on, this is no time for jokes!"

"No, it's true," I said. "I dreamed there was something left in one of the pockets in the coat that Ted wears, so I sent Judy to look for it."

"And did she find something?"

"I'm not sure yet. I haven't had the time to ask her."

He looked around. "Well, where is she?"

"I thought I saw her in the lobby near the court room. Ted might try to call her in as a witness."

He bobbed his head up and down. "We can use that in our favor. Good, good."

It's funny Michael Bonovitch looked like someone out of a movie, pin striped suit, slicked down salt and pepper hair, and a New York accent.

"Well, it's show time." He said as he held the door open for me.

The courtroom was teaming with people, mostly reporters. The girls sat in the back, and Ted and Bill sat at the table next to me. Bill did his best not to make eye contact with me, unlike Ted who glared at me when he took his chair.

"All rise for the honorable Judge Thompson!"

We stopped talking and quickly stood as the judge entered.

"You may be seated."

It was odd sitting there next to Ted and Bill, on opposite sides of this issue, when just nine months ago I was sitting at Ted's dinner table. In the back, next to Judy, were Katrina, Pastor Randolph, and Mark, his son. I could feel the prayers of other brothers and sisters that day. I looked back at Judy. She looked confident and pointed to her purse. I whispered to my lawyer, "She's found something. What should we do?"

"Nothing right now."

"Plaintiff, you may call your first witness."

"Nasheeka Coleman, please take the stand. Raise your right hand. Do you solemnly swear to tell the whole truth and nothing but the truth, so help you God?"

"I do."

"Can you state your name, please?" The attorney asked.

"Nasheeka Coleman."

"How long have you known the defendant?"

"Who?"

"Dr. Clint." The attorney reminded her.

Her eyes found me. "I've come to his office at least three times."

"What kind of doctor is he?"

"He does abortions."

"How many times did you see Dr. Clint?" the attorney asked again.

"Three times: Twice the year before and last September."

"And tell me Miss Coleman, did Dr. Clint ever ask you for any money during any of those visits?"

"Yes!"

"What! That's not true!" I leaned over to my lawyer and whispered it again, "That's not true!"

He placed a steadying hand on my arm. "Just hold on, Clint; we will have our time."

Our attention returned to the girl on the stand. "Yes, and could you tell us what happened?"

"Well, I came to Dr. Clint's office. We were the only ones in the room. The nurse had, umm, left for something. That's when Dr. Clint told me I was having more than one baby and that it would cost more. I was already late in coming for an abortion, and didn't want to wait another day. So I asked him to hand me my purse and I paid him."

"You paid him?"

"Yes! Another $200."

"What did he do with the money?"

"He, umm, put it into his pocket."

The attorney prodded. "Then what happened?"

"The, umm, nurse came back and he did it."

"He did what? The abortion?"

"Yes. The abortion."

"That's all, Your Honor."

"Counsel, do you wish to cross-examine the witness?"

"Yes, Your Honor." My attorney walked forward.

"Miss Coleman, is that correct?"

"Yes."

"Is it true that on two of those visits you couldn't pay Dr. Clint, and promised that you would be back to pay?"

"Umm, I'm not sure. It was so long ago."

"Maybe this will help you remember."

He handed her a sheet. "Do you recognize this paper?"

"Yes, it's a bill."

"And would you read what is written on the bottom of the bill, please?"

"I will come back to pay $100 in full."

My attorney pointed to the page. "Is that your handwriting, Miss Coleman?"

"Yes, it is."

"Are you sure it's your writing?"

"I know my own handwriting."

He turned to the bailiff. "Deputy, could you give this to the judge?"

"And did you come back to pay?"

Her voice was a little lower. "No."

"Speak up please so we all could hear."

"NO!"

"In fact, Miss Coleman, isn't it true that you never paid Dr. Clint anything at all? And you never intended to pay anything this time either?"

Her lawyer piped in. "Objection, your honor! He's leading the witness."

"This is all relevant to the case, your honor."

"Objection overruled. Please continue," the judge said, extending his hand out to Bonovitch.

"I ... umm forgot the question."

"Miss Coleman, isn't it true that you never paid Dr. Clint anything at all? She began to squirm in her seat, "I ... Umm."

"Didn't you tell the secretary that you left your purse in the car and that you would be right back?"

"I, umm, I'm not sure. I was in a lot of pain, you know."

"Miss Coleman, could you read the top of this form, please."

She read, "Office rules."

"And now would you read the second to the last line on this form, please?"

Reluctantly, she read, "At no time will the patient be left alone in the office with the presiding doctor. There will be a nurse present at all times."

"Now, Miss Coleman, I know that it was nine months ago and you said you were in a lot of pain at the time so I will ask the question again. Were you at any time alone with Dr. Clint?"

Her voice quivered. "I, I, I'm not sure. I was in a lot of pain, like I said."

"Objection! Your Honor, he is clearly leading the witness."

"Sustained."

"No more questions, Your Honor."

"Counselor, do you want to redirect at this time?"

Ted and Bill's attorney looked pained. "No, Your Honor."

"You may step down. You may call your next witness."

"The plaintiff calls Tabitha Owens."

"Raise your right hand: Do you solemnly swear to tell the whole truth and nothing but the truth, so help you God?"

"I do."

"You may be seated."

"Tell us your name and how you know Dr. Clint?"

*This is not good. I forgot about Tabitha.*

"Well, I am a receptionist/secretary."

"And how was it, working for the Women's Clinic?"

"It was always busy. A lot of woman came to the clinic."

"As opposed to other clinics? Why is that?"

"Dr. Clint had a way with the woman at the clinic."

"What do you mean by 'a way?'"

"He would take out a lot of women … him and Dr. Bill."

Bill's face turned red. "Were you one of those women?"

"Objection! This is irrelevant. My client's personal life is not on trial here."

"Where are you going with this, counselor?"

"I will show relevancy, Your Honor."

"Objection overruled. Continue."

"Tabitha, were you one of those women …?"

"Yes."

"Tell us what happened."

"Well, Dr. Clint called me back to his office. We had been flirting for most of the day, and he asked me a question."

"What question?"

"He wanted to know how much cash we had taken in that day."

"That's a strange question. How much was taken in?"

"About $2,500."

"What happened after that?"

"Well, we went out to dinner together."

"We, meaning you and Dr. Clint?"

"Yes. Dr. Clint and I went to dinner that night and ..."

"Objection! Your Honor, again, my client's personal business has nothing to do with the case," my attorney insisted.

"It does, Your Honor! May I proceed?"

"Objection overruled. Proceed."

"Okay. You said you went out to dinner that night. What happened next?"

"We were going to his house, but he wanted to stop by the office first."

"Stop by the office?"

"Yes. He said that he had forgotten something." "

Ted and Bill's attorney had a slight smile. "Like the $2,500?"

"Objection!"

"Sustained! Strike that remark. Counselor, watch your comments. You're leading the witness."

"Yes, Your Honor."

"Continue."

"Did Dr. Clint say what it was that he had forgotten?"

"He said it was a phone number of a friend of his."

"And did he come outside holding anything?"

"Yes."

"He did? What was he holding?"

"He was holding a piece of paper."

"And then what happened?"

"Well, he dropped me off at my car."

"Weren't you planning to stay together that night?"

"Yes. That's what I don't understand — something just happened and he wanted to be alone. So I got out of his car and went home. I wasn't happy about it, either."

"What happened when you came to work the next day?"

"Well, when I got to work I was supposed to put together all the funds collected the day before and write them down, but ..."

The attorney prompted, "But what?"

"The drawer was empty and the form was filled out already."

"Was there anybody there at the time?"

"Yes."

"There was? Who?"

"Dr. Ted. So I asked him what had happened, and he said that it was taken care of already. I thought it was odd because it was one of the things I was hired to do."

"It was? Hm-m-m. No more questions, Your Honor."

"Would the defense like to question the witness?"

"Yes, Your Honor."

"Miss Owens, isn't it true that it was you who had very different plans that night, and that it was another doctor you were, in fact, meeting in that parking lot and not my client?"

"I, I, don't know what you mean." She looked like she wanted to race from the room.

"What was the name of the restaurant that you ate at that night, Miss Owens?"

"I think it was Captain's Bell."

"You think? Don't you know?"

"Yes, it was the Captain's Bell."

"Now, why would my client choose this restaurant, since he is allergic to shellfish? So, maybe it was not Dr. Clint who was dining with you that night, now was it?"

She seemed to wilt before my eyes. "No."

"It was a doctor, but it wasn't Dr. Clint, was it?"

She dropped her head and said, "No."

"Who was the doctor that took you out to dinner, who

stopped by the office and then took you to a hotel that night?"

"It was Dr. Ted. We had been meeting together for months while I worked at the office."

"Objection!"

"Sustained! Are there any more questions?"

"No, Your Honor."

"Counselor, do you want to redirect?"

"No, Your Honor."

"Then the court is in recess until 1:30."

"All rise!"

When the judge exited, I immediately turned to my attorney. "Wow, how did you know that she would fold?"

He snapped his briefcase shut. "I didn't."

"But, I whispered, 'I'm allergic to shellfish.'"

"I thought I would take a shot at it and get her to tell us what really happened. I had no idea that she would say what she said."

Without speaking a word to us, Judy found a way to slip us the information that we needed. I handed the sheet to my attorney.

"Let's get some lunch. I think there's a deli downstairs." Katrina found me and came to lunch with us.

"Judy told me she had to testify." Katrina spoke low so no one would over hear.

"That's a good thing for our case. They keep bringing up these people that are making their case weaker. But this paper is going to bust the case wide open."

After lunch we headed back upstairs and that's where we met up with Ted and Bill. The anger was all over Ted's face, and Bill just looked down. For a brief moment, my heart began to ache for my friends and I longed to hear their laughter again. We walked into the courtroom. Seated again, the bailiff walked in.

"All rise!"

Judge Thompson took his seat.

"You may be seated."

"Counselor, you may begin."

"The Defense calls Judith O'Donnell."

Judy made her way to the stand. "Raise your right hand. Do you swear to tell the truth and nothing but the truth, so help you God?"

"I do."

"Please state your name, for the record."

"Judith O'Donnell, but most people call me Judy."

"And Miss O'Donnell, where do you work?"

"I work at the Women's Clinic."

"How long have you been working for the Women's Clinic?"

"Well, I started working for the clinic about five years ago."

"And what is your job at the clinic?"

"I am a receptionist/secretary. I sign in patients, take the payments, and log them in."

"Do you log in all the money?"

"No, sir. I only log in checks, credit cards, and money orders."

"So, do you receive cash payments?"

"Yes, sir."

"But you never log it on the log books?"

"No, sir. I don't."

"About how much cash money comes in a day at the clinic?"

"About $4,000."

"So much? About how many abortions can a clinic this size perform?"

"We do as many as 25-30 a day ... sometimes more. We perform mostly abortions, but women do come in for other reasons."

"Such as?"

"Such as exams and ..."

"Objection! Your Honor, this has nothing to do with the case!"

"Sustained. Get to the point, counselor."

"Go on, Miss O'Donnell."

"As I was saying, we do other types of exams also, but we

mostly focus on abortions."

"Why is that?"

"It brings in more money."

"Who is it that collects all that money and logs it in?"

"Dr. Ted."

"Do you ever see it again?"

"No, he makes the deposits."

"Does anyone go over the records?"

"No, sir."

"Miss O'Donnell, can you read what's on this paper?"

"Yes."

"What is it?"

"It's a receipt for $3,000."

"Is this a receipt that your office gives to patients?"

"No, sir, it is not."

"Can you read what it says at the top, please?"

"Swiss-Karl Bank, Switzerland."

At that moment Ted put his face in his hand.

"Is there anything else on the receipt?"

"Yes."

"What is it?"

"The total next to a name."

"Could you read this to us please?"

"$45,000, and the name is Theodore A. Ryan."

The whole courtroom erupted!

"Order in the court! Order in the court! Any more outbursts like that and I will order the bailiff to clear the courtroom, and this will continue as a closed trial."

"I submit this to the court as Defense Evidence Exhibit A, Your Honor. No more questions."

I looked over at Ted and he had his face in his hands. The courtroom had quieted down.

"Any questions, counselor?"

With a puzzled look on his face, "No, Your Honor."

"The Defense calls Theodore A. Ryan to the stand."

"Raise your right hand. Do you swear to tell the whole truth and nothing but the truth, so help you God?"

"I do." He stared straight ahead.

"Dr. Ted, is that what everyone calls you?"

"Yes."

"And you work where?"

"At the Women's Clinic."

"What type of doctor are you?"

"I perform abortions." Our eyes met. He looked a bit defiant.

"So, during the day you are a doctor, is that correct?"

"Yes." He sat up straighter in his seat.

"Can you speak up, please?"

"YES."

"But something happens after hours, and has been happening for years, now hasn't is? You have been living two very separate lives. One of gambling, drinking, and women."

Ted's face drained of all color.

"Objection!"

"Overruled! Proceed."

"Isn't it correct to state, Mr. Ryan, that for years now, you have been putting away money in a Swiss account?"

He hesitated, but finally answered, "Yes."

"Money you have been gleaning from the money drawer — to take care of your addiction — and putting it into a Swiss bank. The truth is, Dr. Ted, it is not Dr. Clint who was embezzling. It was *you!* Is that true?"

He broke down. "Yes! Yes! Yes! It's true! I only said it was him because he was going to ruin everything we have worked for! When he came back talking that Jesus stuff — and when he walked out — I wanted to get him back! I wanted to ruin him! And that God of his, too!"

"Your Honor, in view of this evidence presented to the court, the Defense requests a directed verdict in favor of the defendant, Dr. Edward Clint."

The place again erupted.

"Order! Order in the court!"

The crowd barely seemed to quiet.

"The court finds in favor of the defendant, Dr. Edward Clint, on the charge of embezzlement: NOT GUILTY. I will entertain countercharges by the defendant against the plaintiff at a later date. Court dismissed!"

I leapt from my seat. Katrina raced to me. I hugged her hard. Then I turned to my attorney.

"Thank you so much!" I shook his hand. "God bless you."

The news crews went crazy. In fact, everyone was gathering around asking questions.

I saw Bill over by the corner, just sitting there. I walked over to him after the courtroom was empty. "Bill, I told you earlier that I will always be your friend."

He shook his head. "It's over. Just like that; it's over. I've worked so hard. All I wanted was to be the best pediatrician ever. My wife, my practice gone — all of it gone. What else do I have to live for?"

"Bill, I lost everything, too: My practice, my reputation ... but I found Jesus in all this mess."

Bill shook his head again. "But what is He to me? I've done too much. You know how much we were making off each one of those dollars with a little fingerprint on them!"

"Bill, don't you know that God already knows? And if you repent of everything, He will forgive you. Would you like to pray and ask Him to do that?"

Bill studied his hands. He finally looked up at me. "Yes, I would."

So, right there in the courtroom, I walked Bill through the "sinner's prayer." Oh, the tears and the rejoicing that followed.

Bill came to the meeting the following night and he brought his wife. She said that there was such a big change in him that she had to come see for herself about this Jesus.

"Pastor Randolph, this is my friend Bill Summerbell and his wife, Evelyn."

"Very glad to meet you."

"Thank you!"

"Clint has mentioned both of you to me a few times before. He loves and respects you both very much."

"Excuse me a minute."

I left them talking, and walked over to Katrina and Aaron, who were chatting. I hugged them both, and was very happy to see that Aaron was on the worship team now.

"I'm learning more and more about you every day, Aaron. I had no idea you were so good on the guitar."

"Ah-h, somebody had to play at the Bar Mitzvahs."

We all laughed. He gestured to the sound system. "I've got to help put away the equipment. Would you excuse me?"

"No problem." I said then turned to Katrina.

"How's my favorite doctor?" Katrina asked with a smile.

I wanted to grab her in my arms, but I knew we had not made the big announcement just yet; so I got away with a quick hug. "I saw that Bill came with his wife. How did they like it?"

"They both really hit it off with Pastor Randolph. It turns out that they were born in the same state." We both laughed.

"Katrina, I know that I have one more thing to do."

"What is that, Clint?"

I paused for a moment, "To visit my father in jail."

"Jail? Why is he in jail?"

Tears began to fill my eyes. "Katrina, this is a part of my life I have not told anybody about. In fact, most of that information was lost in my childhood memories. I grew up in a house where my dad would beat my mom. Sometimes he would beat on her so bad that she would sit for days in the dark, so I would not see the marks on her body. My aunt would be our only rescue, and, in fact, she prayed for us all the time. Mom would leave Dad and then go back; leave and go back. Each time the beatings grew worse and worse. One day, after a really bad fight, I ran and hid in back of the house. I heard shots ring out, and then Dad drove off really fast. I found my mom on the floor in a pool of blood. I was 9 years old then. I went into foster care and the people who took care of me sent me to the best schools. That's why I am 'Doctor Clint' today."

"Wow, Clint, I had no idea."

"I want to go to see my dad and let him know that I forgive him ... and tell him about Jesus."

She studied me. "Do you think he will listen?"

"I don't know, but I have to try."

"Do you know where he is?"

"I'm not sure, but I have a feeling it has something to do with the envelope my aunt gave me. We have a lot to talk about, and I want Pastor Randolph to be there, too."

"What about tomorrow at 11 at Mama's? I will reserve a corner booth."

"Perfect."

"I hate this part."

"What part?" I asked.

"The part where we must say goodbye."

I wished I could pull her close. "I, umm, know the feeling."

We stood in silence for just a beat, as if neither wanted to utter the words.

"Good night," I finally said with a longing look in my eyes.

# CHAPTER 12

## The Big News Goes Public

I could hardly sleep, so I opened the manila envelope that Aunt Deb gave to me. Inside was a letter. It read: "My Dear Edward, by the time you read this letter I will be with the Lord and watching you from heaven. It does my heart good to know that you, too, love Jesus and that one day soon we will meet again. Now, my estate is listed below:

1. In these countries do I own property: England, France, Italy, and Switzerland. If you would like to sell those properties you may, but please pay the servants handsomely.

2. In the United States do I own property in Washington, DC, Washington State, Maine, North and South Carolina, Virginia, Texas, Utah, Florida, and California."

*Aunt Deb was loaded!* She had stocks in everything. She was helping outreach ministries everywhere, and the list she gave me went on and on. I had no idea what to do with all this money and stuff. Her bank account, let me say, *one* of her bank accounts was loaded! I needed "Jesus wisdom" to know just what I should do with all this stuff. "Lord, you know my heart is not toward all this money, so protect me and lead me. Amen."

The list went on and on. Then at the bottom of the page was a note that read: "My Edward, as to the whereabouts of your father, he is in the Richmond, Virginia Prison serving a life sentence."

I knew that I had one more thing to do, and I knew it would be the hardest thing I had to ever do. I take that back: Letting go of my mother's hand that day was the hardest thing I had to do ... but this was a close second. "Lord, should I go?"

Silence.

"Lord, should I go to see my father and tell him about You?"

Nothing.

I waited; still nothing. Does His silence mean "no" or "wait"?

I put it aside and went to sleep. Later I woke up in a panic! What a bad dream! Sweat was pouring off of me; my pillow was wet and the sheets had wrapped themselves all around me. It seemed so real: I was coming to see my dad at the prison. When I got inside, the door that I had come in by disappeared ... and it was only high walls. I could hear my dad's voice saying, "Is that you?"

Then I saw his hand reach up, so I knew where he was. I jumped up to climb the wall, but when I did that, he turned into a Rottweiler. It was very vicious and bit me. He let go and then I woke up. "Oh, Lord, what was that all about? Should I not go?"

*I will wait on the Lord and see what He wants me to do. Until then, I will get rested up for tomorrow.*

I was up early, spending time with the Lord. It was there in the stillness of my heart that I heard, "Go."

I knew what that meant and I asked, "When, Lord, when should I go?"

"Tomorrow."

I called Katrina. The phone rang.

"Hello?"

"I couldn't help calling you. When I'm with you, Katrina, time stands still. I do, however, need to tell you something."

"OK?" I could hear the apprehension in her voice.

"I had an aunt who recently died. I'm her only living relative. That's what I've been doing, tying up loose ends. She's left me everything' so to speak."

"Oh, Clint, I am sorry. You spoke so highly of Aunt Deb."

"Yeah, that was a hard one. Thank God I have you and Mama. Anyhow, she was very wealthy."

"Very wealthy?" "Let's just say that our grandchildren won't have to work ever."

"You're kidding, right?"

"I'm glad I'm not."

"Oh, Clint, you will need to hear from God for wisdom. Have you spoken to Pastor Randolph?"

"Not yet. I'll call him after I talk with you."

"Look, don't say anything to anyone. I don't want to look differently in front of anybody's eyes."

"No problem. I will keep it in my prayers."

"I love you so much."

"Say it to me one more time."

"I love you."

"And I love you, too."

Comfortable silence fell between us.

"Do you need someone to ride with you to see your dad?"

"Thanks for the offer, but I need to walk this one alone ... and I know it won't be easy."

"What time will you be leaving?"

"About 4:30 Monday morning."

"That's tomorrow, why so early?"

"It's a long way and I want to be prayed up by the time I get there. I will talk to you on the way back to let you know how it went."

CHAPTER 13

# God Gives Dad
# Another Chance

I arrived home, and a message from Montgomery said that we needed to meet about Aunt Deb's estate and to give him a call on Monday afternoon. My heart sank. I lay on the carpet before the living God, knowing that He was just waiting for me to come to Him. I labored in tears before God — I don't know how many hours, for sure — but I woke up the next morning still on the carpet. I arose and took a shower, got dressed and headed to Richmond Prison.

At the prison I was searched by the guards to see if I was carrying something to give the prisoners. I wasn't even allowed to carry my Bible. That surprised me. The sound of the iron doors closing behind me was chilling. I waited for some time, and then I was taken into a room with a window. There was a phone near it. In walked a gray- haired man. He was weathered, but medium height like me. He sat down and picked up the phone. "So, that's how you turned out. You look like her. I never thought you were mine because you never looked like me."

I never realized he doubted I was his child. But I pushed that from my mind.

"I, I didn't know you were here until now."

He sneered. "Who told you? It was that religious sister of hers, wasn't it?"

"You mean Aunt Deb? Yes, she told me how to get in touch with you."

"Why you want to see me? I killed your mama!"

"I, I wanted to tell you that you can find forgiveness in Jesus."

His eyes narrowed. "Don't come in here preachin' to me, boy! I don't need your weak God! He ain't never cared for me, and He don't much care now!"

"No, Dad, you are mistaken! He does care for you! God's been telling me for years about His love for you. That's what I came to tell you."

"Let me tell you something, boy! That night your mother was trying to preach that same religious stuff to me, so I slapped her! But she kept saying that she forgives me and that Jesus loves me. With every slap, she wouldn't stop. So,

I took the gun and shot her. I cursed her and I cursed her God."

"I know the story, Dad, about what happened. I was there, remember?"

He seemed to spit out the words. "Yes, I remember. It was your story that nailed it for me in court!"

"Dad, you can be free even behind these bars if you give your life to Jesus."

He started laughing. "You will be full of regrets if you turn Jesus away now, Dad."

"You listen to me, boy! The only thing I regret about that night is that I didn't shoot you, too! To hell with your religion. I don't need no God."

He laughed again. I just shook my head. Then I put the phone down and got up and walked away.

I didn't let him see me cry, but the guard did and he said to me, "Look, man, don't take it to heart. Man, this dude is eaten up with bitterness, but what you said to him touched my heart. If Jesus was willing to forgive a murderer like him, what about me, man?"

"If you repent of your sins — that means not walking in them again, and give Jesus your whole life — yes, even you."

"I don't think that you have any time to, uh, help me do that."

"I have all the time in the world."

I didn't leave Richmond until late that evening. What a bittersweet pill that was. It was about 2 a.m. before I even got home. I had called Montgomery on the way to Richmond and found out that Aunt Deb was cremated. He said that that they were shipping her ashes to me on Monday, and asked what he should do with the other estates. I asked him if there was a home that he wanted, and told him it would be his for being a faithful friend and lawyer.

"I will give that some thought, and be in touch on Monday."

That was that!

# CHAPTER 14

# 'The Wedding and Beyond ...'

Iknew it was too late to call Katrina, so I held off until later. As soon as I finished my prayer time the next morning, I called her. "Hello? Clint, is everything all right? I got worried when I didn't hear anything."

"So much happened yesterday. My dad is a bitter old man who will end up in hell if he doesn't receive Jesus."

"So, I take it that it didn't go well?"

"I went up there thinking that he would be happy to see me, and would repent and receive Jesus. But he just cursed me, laughed at me and about killing my mom. I told him of the love that Jesus has for him, even in his anger.

"He said that the night that my mother died, she was telling him about Jesus and that's why he shot her."

"Wow, Clint, I am sorry."

"I'm not. I learned an important part about a missing piece of my life: I will see my mom again!"

"What do you mean?"

"The last thing she was doing was sharing about Jesus."

"Wow, Clint, I didn't think about that. That's great!"

"God didn't let me leave from there like that: When I left, one of the guards heard me talking with my dad and he received Jesus. I spent most of the evening with him when he got off work. That's why I didn't call you."

"Wow! You did have a lot happen."

"And on top of all that, I have to handle my Aunt Deb's ashes on Monday."

"Oh, Clint." Katrina said.

I quickly added, "She and Mom are back together again and that is comforting. Look, can I see you?"

"Sure, when?"

"Now."

Now she laughed, "You know it will take you at least 15 minutes to get to my house!"

"Then in 15 minutes, see you soon." I hung up the phone and jumped into my car. I found I like my Toyota better than the Mercedes I used to drive. There she was standing outside in her white shorts and red and white striped shirt. I got out of the car and embraced her.

"Wow you did miss me!"

"Look, can we get married soon?"

"How soon?" I could hear the surprise in her voice.

"Today!"

She chuckled. "Today? That's crazy! I have to get my bridesmaids and everything."

"Okay, how about tomorrow?"

"Clint, how about in two months? That will be in September. That's my birthday month anyway. Okay?"

"Okay, I will wait until then, but it's not going to be easy. You plan the wedding of your dreams, have as many bridesmaids as you want, whatever you want as many as you want. It will be paid for no matter what it costs."

"Oh, Clint, I love you!"

"Say it again!"

"I love you."

I jump into my car.

Surprised, she said, "Where are you going?"

"I've got to go get something!" I'll see you for lunch with Pastor Randolph, be there at 1."

"That's only 45 minutes," she called out.

"Bring Mama, too. It concerns her."

Katrina, Mama, and Pastor Randolph were seated at a table in the back waiting for me.

"Wow you clean up good," Katrina said with a smile, I had gone and put on a clean shirt and nice pair of pants.

"Welcome," said Pastor Randolph. We shook hands.

Mama gave me this big ole' hug. "Lord, Clint, is everything all right?"

"Yes, Mama I wanted to talk you," I paused, "Mama, as you know, I have been spending quite a bit of time with your daughter, and I have enjoyed every moment."

Mama smiled and patted Katrina's hand. "Yes, I've noticed. She is a good girl."

I look at Pastor Randolph with a smile. "Well Mama I want to ask you if I may marry Katrina and make her my wife?"

"Lord, Clint, you want to marry my baby?"

"With all of my heart."

"What do you feel Katrina? About marrying Dr. Clint? You ready, child?"

Katrina looked at me with the warmest smile. "Yes, Mama I am, with all of my heart."

"Then I say yes, you may marry her!"

So I got down on one knee in front of Katrina, with her ring and said, "Katrina, I have loved you for a long time now and each time I have to leave you my heart aches to be with you again. So with that said, would you make me the happiest man on earth and consent to be my wife?"

"Yes, with all my heart! Yes, I will be honored to be Mrs. Edward Clint!"

I placed the ring on her finger — a 3-karat blue sapphire surrounded with diamond clusters.

She showed her ring to her mother and as she did I spoke up and said, "There is one more thing."

Katrina smiled.

"Mama, I will be able to take good care of your daughter and you, too," I said.

"Clint I know you will take care of my baby. You'll find a good job and—"

"I had an aunt die and leave me with everything because she had no children," I politely stepped in. "Let's just say, Mama, your grandchildren won't have to work."

Mama almost fainted when she heard about the inheritance. We got her some cold water and she was fine. It's funny how things work out. God is so good!

The next few weeks I only saw Katrina a few times while she was planning the wedding,

During one of those times she told me the wedding theme. "Guess what the theme of the wedding is?" she said excitedly.

I smiled at her, "What?"

With a big grin she quickly answered, "Paris!"

"I didn't know they had themes. Wow that sounds great!"

She looked at her watch, "Oooh, I've got to go! I'm meeting Danielle and Judy at 3 p.m. I've got to go. You don't mind, do you?"

"No, of course not. You go plan. I'll have a lifetime with you."

We embraced and she was off again.

She and Judy were always out and about with Danielle. Danielle was the best of the best and had a knack for making wedding dreams come true.

I called Katrina up and asked to see her and her wedding planner at Mama's Place. "Bring Judy, too."

"Sure, Clint, is everything all right?" she sounded a little worried.

"More then all right, and besides, I miss you." I could hear her smile.

"We found my dress today," she said with a playful sassiness that was alluring to my heart.

"You did? You sure you don't want to get married today?"

"She laughed. "I'm sure. Look, we will see you in about 30 minutes."

"How about 29 minutes?" I sounded playful.

She laughed. "Oh, Clint!"

Sure enough, in walked three giggly women. "It's 28 minutes and we are early," Katrina announced.

I laughed and hugged Katrina and then Judy and Danielle. "Please have a seat, ladies."

"I don't want to take up too much of your time but I had an idea. How does Paris sound?"

"How does Paris sound for what?" Katrina asked. "For the honeymoon?"

"For the wedding, the guests, the honeymoon, and a week of sightseeing. Everything!"

Katrina placed her hand over her mouth. "You're kidding, right?"

I looked at her. "Invite 60 or 70 of your friends and family. For the ones who don't go, we will have a big dinner the week before we go. What do you think?"

I turned to the planner. "Danielle?"

All the women erupted into high-pitched squeals and applause.

"So Danielle, you got your hands full. Do you think you

can handle it? You've only a month and a half, if you need more time," I chuckled. "Which I hope not. I don't think I can wait that long, but if you do just let me know. Contact me as soon as you can, okay?"

"Okay, Clint, no problem. I am so excited!"

"Oh and Danielle, ask your husband to come. I would love to meet him."

I stood. "Look, I won't stop you ladies from your planning. I will see you later." I kissed Katrina's hand and was off, leaving them abuzz with excitement.

•

The day did come and the dinner was at the Hilton Hotel in Washington, D.C. We had 150 guests. The whole room was transformed into Paris. In the corner was the base of the Eiffel Tower and around the perimeter of the room were what looked like little shops. Each table had on it large elephant leaves and a bouquet of cream roses that sat next to a small, tiered cake. It was amazing! The waiters looked French, and the menu was French with English print. Danielle had not missed a thing. She paid attention to every little detail. Softly in the background violin music played. It was perfect.

Katrina looked as if she walked out of a magazine. She wore a long, teal hand-dyed couture dress that seemed to flow in both beauty and style.

I went to Danielle and said, "You have outdone yourself today."

She looked at me with a smile and said, "Oh really? Wait until the wedding. You haven't seen anything yet!"

The dinner was amazing and those who could not go to Paris felt as if they had been there.

•

The time finally came for the trip to Paris. We all were very excited. Well, maybe not Mama — she had never been on a plane before.

We had a private plane. Katrina and Mama sat next to me. I wasn't sure if Mama was going to make it, but we all made it just fine. We arrived at the Four Seasons Hotel of Paris, France in the late afternoon. I enjoyed watching Katrina and our family and friends as they walked out of the airport. It was priceless because most of them had never been out of their own city. The entry of the hotel was breathtaking. It had beautiful tapestry and white marble statues on each side of the room leading to the front desk, and a grand chandelier hanging over marble flooring. Danielle had arranged suites for the guests, which had fresh flowers and chocolates inside every room. She piped in.

"May I have everyone's attention, please?" she said. "Here is the itinerary that's planned for our trip. I only ask that in honor of our host that we be on time for each time we come together. In each envelope you will find your room key and other information. It is now 3:30 p.m. Hors d'oeuvres and drinks will be served between 5:30 and 6:30. So you have time to unpack and relax. We will see you then."

Katrina, her mom and Judy shared a suite while I shared one with Mark. Aaron and Isaiah shared a room and Pastor Randolph had the suite across the hall from them. Just six more days until the wedding and then I'd be off with my bride to one of the houses that Aunt Deb had left me in the countryside of France.

During the break I shared with Pastor Randolph the surprise gift I was giving everyone. "Wow that is incredible. Are you sure about this, Clint?"

"More than sure. I've already made the provision and will present it to them all at dinner tonight. I want our guests to go shopping and freely taste and experience France."

"Clint, does Katrina know?" he asked.

"No, not yet. This is my gift to her: to bless the people she holds dear to her heart."

"So mum's the word with me!" Pastor laughed out loud.

"Oh, I've taken care of the legal paperwork for the wedding. So don't worry about that," I said.

"That's great. Don't want a piece of paper to stand in the way of love, now do you?"

We laughed. "Hey, what do you think about Isaiah?"

Pastor Randolph shook his head. "He is totally amazing. We are spending our time together opening the Word, and

I'm truly honored to know him. The wealth of wisdom that flows from him is truly amazing."

I patted his shoulders and said, "I agree. I totally agree."

"Look, time to get dressed for dinner I've got to get these envelopes to Danielle before it starts so she can get them to the waiters to pass out to our guests."

"Great touch!"

I walked around with my bride to be, hand-in-hand. "You're glowing, you know." I stared at her.

She blushed. "I am? That's because this all feels like a dream. Look at this room! Gold candle chandeliers, all these mirrors on the wall with the most gorgeous tapestries, and look, Clint!"

She pointed to the flowers that were in tall, clear vases. "The pink and coral roses and then the small purple flowers at our cocktail tables. Oh, Clint, this is perfect!"

I looked at her and said, "I have a surprise for you."

"You do?" her eyes brightened. "What is it?"

"You'll find out at dinner." She pouted and I almost told her, but I was saved by Danielle coming in gathering folks for dinner.

We all walked into the first very intimate dining room. We could feel the excitement as oohs and ahhs erupted. It was beautiful. Katrina placed her hand over her mouth in disbelief." Look at all the gold crown molding and the gold and silver chairs. Oh, Clint, all the tables are draped in long French colonial style and the pink, red, and floral center pieces! It's beautiful!"

Danielle piped in, "May we have the wedding party please sit at table one. Everyone else, feel free to sit down where you like."

Everyone ordered their food and drinks and enjoyed each other's company. After dessert I stood up and tapped my glass to get everyone's attention. A silence came over the room.

"First of all, I want to say thank you for each of you being an intimate part of Katrina's and my life," I said, motioning to Danielle. "If Danielle could pass out the cards to each guest, please."

She beckoned to the waiter. She handed out some on one side of the room, while the waiter did so on the other. "Please don't open them yet until everyone gets one and when you have one, hold it up in the air," I said.

I finally could see that everyone had one, including Danielle and her husband. "Okay, Katrina this is my gift to you. I know that blessing your family and friends blesses you, so I have just given each person $2,000 to use as they shop and play in Paris!"

The room erupted with excited voices, as everyone scrambled to look into the envelopes. Katrina gave me the biggest hug, "Oh, Clint! Oh Clint, I love you so much! Thank you!"

Danielle had plans for Katrina and me, pre-wedding photo shoots in different places in France, and sweet lunches. She even had tours planned for anyone who wanted to go. The spa was open to anyone who wanted to experience a time of relaxation. The days seemed to fly.

Finally, wedding day arrived! For some reason, I was nervous. Pastor Randolph prayed over me, and I could feel peace again. We were finally dressed and it was time to go to the great room. I could hear the violins and the cellos. I walked into the room. It had an arch of white flowers and lace dripping with green vines all over; it looked as if we were in a vineyard at twilight. The mother of the bride entered and sat, and then the bridesmaids came in hand-dyed coral venture dresses that flowed like waves to the floor.

Then the music changed. And in walked Katrina. She was the most wonderful bride I had ever seen. Her brown skin in her off-white dress took my breath away. I couldn't take my eyes off of her. Her hair was pulled up with strands that fell on her shoulders. Her bridesmaids were Judy — the maid of honor — and her girlfriends Pearl and Analea. My best man was Mark and both of Katrina's brothers were groomsmen.

Pastor Randolph and Isaiah presided over the wedding. Our first kiss was when Pastor Randolph said, "You may kiss the bride."

As I held my new bride in my arms, I could not help but

think about the life I had before she came into it. My life was in shambles then, and I didn't even know it. I had been going along for years, denying the pain of my youth. I had wrapped my heart in ice, never daring to embrace much emotion. In fact, the biggest denial of emotion was the fact that I had made it my life's work to kill babies, stealing their lives before they could even get here.

And for the longest, that had been all right with me. I had been making good money, driving nice cars, eating at the best restaurants. But God worked a miracle in my heart. He helped me see that I wanted no part in the spilling of innocent blood. He gave me a new heart and a new life in him. And that would have been enough — I am so grateful for the changes He has worked in me over the past year. But God gave me something more. He also gave me love.

And now I get the chance to start a whole new life with the woman who helped me see that my heart could smile. I squeezed her around the waist as we turned to see our loved ones for the first time as husband and wife.

•

After the wedding celebration, we rode off in a carriage pulled by white horses, with the release of white doves.

As we rode off, I asked my new bride, "How do you feel about mission work?"

She smiled and said, "Sure, I would love it. Where to?"

"What do you think about China?"

# Epilogue

"So much has happened to me in such a short time! God has done great things in my life: He gave me the most beautiful, kindest and, by far, the sweetest woman in the world."

"I think you're a little biased," I wrapped my arms around Katrina as we looked at the garden from the window of our country home. Katrina leaned her head back upon my chest and asked, "What do you think is going to happen with Ted?"

"I'm not sure, really. He has a hearing in a month to find out. There is a possibility that if he checks into a rehab and does some community service, the charges will be dropped."

"Really? Poor Peggy, how will she manage? We will help them, won't we?"

"We think alike. I will always be 'Uncle Clint' to their kids."

"Then what about Bill; isn't he in danger, too?"

"Not really; he didn't know that Ted was stealing from him. And besides he has already closed down the women's clinic and is going back into pediatrics."

"I bet the media is having a field day with that one!"

"You'd think so, but it has been strangely quiet."

"Clint, I want you to read something."

I pulled away to look into her face. "What? My heart?"

"No, silly, I already know what that is saying."

"Really?" I squeezed her a little tighter. She smiled, and then wiggled loose. "Someone special wanted me to give this to you."

She handed me an envelope. I opened it. The handwriting was familiar. It read: "My dear friend, Yeshua has changed my life! I am teaching the 60 'converts' that came up to me that wonderful night in my conference. And I want to say 'thank you' for being so bold. I am proud of you, my son. Marrying you along with your pastor was the delight of my heart.' May the Lord watch between me and thee, while we are absent one from another. Amen. Until we meet again enjoy this part of life, while you have the strength.' Isaiah."

*Wow.* I choked up. "Thank you." I looked at Katrina. "When did he give this to you?"

She smiled, "On the way out the door, when he hugged me. He is so amazing."

"Yes, he is. But you are *more* amazing!" I looked at her big eyes. She put her hand on my face.

"How so?"

"You forgave me for the abortion I performed on you years ago, and then prayed with me to know Jesus.

"You know Clint, I believe that we will see my little one again ... in heaven!"

I embraced Katrina tightly, overwhelmed by her love ... and the love of God in her life!

*"These six things the LORD hates, yes, seven are an abomination to Him ... hands that shed **innocent blood**."*
Proverbs 6:16,17

**If you've been touched by an abortion, then God wants you to know He loves you. Let Him know how you feel. Pray this prayer for yourself and for others:**

"Heavenly Father, I thank you for showing me Your Truth about the sanctity of life. I give to you, Jesus, my life, my heart and my will; be my Savior and Lord. I repent for all the ways that I have condoned the shedding of innocent blood — either directly or indirectly. Lord, forgive me. Now I understand the seriousness of this matter, and confess that this bloodshed is grievous in your eyes.

"Only your blood can clean me of this innocent blood – for their blood cries out to you from the ground. Use me to tell Your Truth, compelled by Your Love. Lord, I thank you for Your Forgiveness, and for cleansing me from all those whose lives were taken innocently because I said nothing. May we be reunited with them someday.

"As I walk in repentance and forgiveness, I walk in your freedom. I pray that you open the eyes and the hearts of others who are walking in this sin. Oh, Lord, do so quickly. In the name of Jesus. Amen."

If you prayed this prayer and need someone to talk to email us at letsprosper2@gmail.com. Someone will get back to you within 48 hours.

# About the Author

Sultana Jones was born and raised in Washington, DC, and has lived there (or in a nearby suburb) her entire life. She is a painter, a musician, an advocate for the less fortunate, a Christian, and a writer. Stories and novels pour from her heart in dreams! It is her calling.

Sultana currently lives near DC with her husband, two children, her brother and Simon, her Chihuahua.

New stories are still finding their place inside of her heart.

# For Ordering My Book

For more information or to purchase additional copies of this book, please visit http://christianreading.com/sjones, or email me at letsprosper2@gmail.com.